NATURAL HISTORY

ALSO BY ANDREA BARRETT

Archangel

The Air We Breathe

Servants of the Map

The Voyage of the Narwhal

Ship Fever

The Forms of Water

The Middle Kingdom

Secret Harmonies

Lucid Stars

NATURAL
HISTORY

stories

ANDREA BARRETT

W. W. NORTON & COMPANY
Independent Publishers Since 1923

Copyright © 2022 by Andrea Barrett

For information about permission to reproduce selections from this book, write to Permissions, W. W. Norton & Company, Inc., 500 Fifth Avenue, New York, NY 10110

For information about special discounts for bulk purchases, please contact W. W. Norton Special Sales at specialsales@wwnorton.com or 800-233-4830

Manufacturing by Lake Book Manufacturing
Book design by Beth Steidle
Production manager: Beth Steidle

ISBN 978-1-324-03519-0

W. W. Norton & Company, Inc., 500 Fifth Avenue, New York, N.Y. 10110
www.wwnorton.com

W. W. Norton & Company Ltd., 15 Carlisle Street, London W1D 3BS

1 2 3 4 5 6 7 8 9 0

for Emily Forland,
stalwart companion

There were some advantages about being a writer of histories. The desk was a shelter one could hide behind, it was a hole one could creep into.

—WILLA CATHER, *The Professor's House*

CONTENTS

I

Wonders of the Shore

3

The Regimental History

31

Henrietta and Her Moths

77

The Accident

95

Open House

121

II

Natural History

153

Author's Note and Acknowledgments

191

I

WONDERS OF THE SHORE

I.

The sea-shore, with its stretches of sandy beach and rocks, seems, at first sight, nothing but a barren waste, merely the natural barrier of the ocean. But to the observant eye these apparently desolate reaches are not only teeming with life, they are also replete with suggestions of the past. They are the pages of a history full of fascination for one who has learned to read them.

The cover is a faded olive, not flashy; not the first thing you'd pull from a bookshelf. *Wonders of the Shore.* Black type, black decorations: a small silhouette of a fiddler crab; a pair of stylized starfish bracketing the author's name. Coiled snails frame the "Wonder" while sea anemones frame the "Shore." Actually it *is* attractive, in a sober, subtle way. Someone labored over that design. And over the photographs, too, reprinted from many sources but freshly labeled and crowded on thick, glossy paper, which makes the book heavy.

The writing is old-fashioned, more detailed than we're used to now; it was published in 1889. The author, Daphne Bannister, thanks a long list of people at the end of her preface. Some are professors at places like Harvard and Barnard, others curators or—the women—assistants at the Smithsonian. Especially thanked are Celia Thaxter, "whose kind invitations to Thaxter Cottage made my working visits to the Hotel such a pleasure," and "my dear friend and stalwart companion, Miss Henrietta Atkins."

One of Henrietta's relatives, Rose Marburg, inherited the book, but for a long time Rose didn't look at it.

II.

It is hoped that this book will suggest a new interest and pleasure to many, and that it will serve as a practical guide to this branch of natural history, without necessitating serious study. Marine organisms are interesting acquaintances when once introduced, and the real purpose of the author is to present, to the latent naturalist, friends whom he will enjoy.

Celia Thaxter is easy to trace; she wrote a book of poems, a collection of pieces about the beloved island where she was raised, a book about her garden. There are letters, too, and portraits and photographs, and a couple of biographies. Among her well-known friends were Whittier, Sarah Orne Jewett, and the painters William Morris Hunt and Childe Hassam. Nathaniel Hawthorne visited her island cottage. Major Greely claimed her poems comforted him during his disastrous Arctic voyage. She met Dickens and Robert Browning.

Daphne, who wrote under two different names, is harder to classify, but she had her day as well and people in the village noticed her: a woman, visiting repeatedly, traveling on her own. At the drugstore, at the theater. Walking along the lake with her friend, pale hair improbably thick above her sharp features and delicate neck. Or skating—she had tiny feet but was very fast—in a costume showing more leg than was usual in this part of upstate New York. Some were annoyed by her manners. After one visit, the *Crooked Lake Gazette* reported:

> Among those arriving last week by train from Bath was Miss Daphne Bannister, here for one of her frequent stays with our esteemed biology teacher, Miss Henrietta Atkins. A well-known authoress, Miss Bannister has written guides to the insect pests, the wildflowers of Massachusetts (where she makes her home), and the birds of the fields and farms. She traveled from the Cornell campus, where she presented a talk on parasitic nematodes.

That one, the gossips said. Henrietta's friend. All around Crooked Lake, people were aware of Henrietta. Mention of her in the *Gazette* goes back as far as grade school: "Winner of the Spelling Bee." "Student Fossil Collection Impresses Visitors." "Sisters Show Off Lake Trout Caught in Fishing Derby." Later articles note her departure for Oswego, where she went for her teacher training, and the grant she received when she finished. She met Daphne after she graduated, at a summer school for the study of natural history run by Louis Agassiz. After that she came back home to teach biology at the high school. She established the Natural History Club, the Young Lepidopterists Club, an ice-skating group, a reading group. Several times she won teaching awards. Each year she pulled a few promising students into her investigations, which ranged from aiding the local farmers' experiments with breeding cows and corn, to studies of fish, the development of other uses for wine grapes during Prohibition, and a new method for producing the membrane used to make balloons and rigid airships impermeable to gas.

All of this is noted in the *Gazette*. Henrietta, so firmly rooted wherever she stands that she looks tall unless she's next to someone else, ages silently in the photographs; her skirts narrow, then rise, then give way to voluminous slacks. Her sleeves are always pushed back from her sturdy wrists and blunt-fingered hands, lines appearing as her hair grays and metamorphoses from a mass pinned at the back of her head to a neat crop just below her ears. Grateful students mention her as they in turn appear in the newspaper for one thing or another. Appreciative colleagues thank her as they retire. The tone is invariably kind—except for the notes about Daphne's visits, which are colored by something that wouldn't be there if either of the women had married. Now they seem to point at something. They might not have read that way then.

III.

Every coast-line shows the destructive effects of the sea, for the bays and coves, the caves at the bases of the cliffs, the buttresses and needles, are the work of the waves. And this work is constantly going on. The knotty sticks so commonly seen on the beach are often the hearts of oak or cedar trees from which the tiny crystals of sand have slowly cut away their less solid outer growth.

In August of 1885, Henrietta was thirty-three and had been teaching high school for twelve years. Although her sister, Hester, was almost a decade younger, she'd married two years earlier and left Henrietta alone at home with their mother. This had suited Henrietta very well until her friend Mason Perrotte, an ambitious farmer whom she'd known for some time, began to court her attentively. Confusingly. Now, after seven months of thinking one way about this in the morning and another in the afternoon, she knew he was about to propose. She was fond of him, as was her mother. If she was going to change her life and start a family, it was surely time. But to leave her job, after all she'd put into it—no point to that unless she could do more work, not less, as Daphne had after leaving her own teaching job. And her mother's argument that Henrietta would be teaching her *own* children wasn't wholly convincing.

She and Daphne had shared a vacation every summer since they'd met, which didn't always mean Daphne visiting Henrietta: sometimes Henrietta went to the little town in western Massachusetts where Daphne, having pried herself free from her parents and her brothers, had bought herself a tiny white house. And twice they'd managed to stay at a resort. Once in the White Mountains, once in Rhode Island: what luxury, to have their meals cooked and their rooms cleaned! Henrietta had been Daphne's guest both times, which might have been awkward if, instead of pointing out that the income she made from her books was much greater than Henrietta's small salary, Daphne had not insisted graciously that those books wouldn't exist without Henrietta's help, so the treat was simply Henrietta's due. This year, having done especially well, Daphne had offered three weeks at the hotel on Appledore Island, a few miles off the New Hampshire coast.

On the day before Henrietta began her journey to the island, Mason came from his farm in Pulteney with a tin of gingersnaps for the train ride and a big white canvas hat that tied with two strips of muslin under her chin. He was wearing the blue-checked shirt he knew she particularly liked. She could feel him trying to get her alone, but instead she sat steadfastly with her mother at the table, making lists of what she should bring and what she would read during this stretch of uninterrupted time. She'd been catching up with Darwin's work since Daphne first led her, years ago, to an acceptance of his great theory. Reading slowly and carefully as her interest deepened, filling pages with notes, repeating some of his experiments and adapting them for her students. But there was no catching up to Daphne.

Daphne wrote to Darwin, and was answered. Daphne wrote to Asa Gray. Daphne wrote about climbing plants and burrowing spiders, publishing more and more articles and then a book, and another and another, earning enough money from those (and also from the part of her writing life she kept quiet) to stop teaching at the academy where she'd been working when they met. Henrietta fell even further behind. Not giving up; but working more slowly than she wished. Only in the summers could she pursue her own investigations wholeheartedly, keeping the thread alive during the school year by stealing an hour or two at night, after her lessons were prepared.

Her "work"—what did she mean by that, exactly? In the libraries of central New York, you can find files of the horticultural and agricultural society bulletins so popular toward the end of the nineteenth century. The *New York Agricultural Experiment Station Bulletin*. The *Rural New-Yorker*. The *Bulletin of the Buffalo Naturalists' Field Club*. The *Western New York Horticultural Society Bulletin*. *Transactions of the New-York State Agricultural Society*. In them are accounts of meetings and county fairs; brief observations about local growing conditions, new seeds and breeds, keeping a clean dairy; longer articles too, weaving multiple sources and reports into an overview for the farmer. Daphne was writing pieces like that when she and Henrietta met; now Henrietta wrote them. "The White Grub of the May Beetle." One or two a year, carefully observed, clearly written, thoughtfully and thoroughly referenced. Useful to students and farmers alike. Together they give a sense of her steady progress through the years, although they don't suggest the work she did with and for Daphne. There's a hint of that in a letter she wrote to Mason during the first week of her stay at Appledore Island:

> Already we've settled into a pleasant routine. Our rooms are on the third floor, mine a few doors down from Daphne's: hers larger than mine, of course, as she needs space for her specimens, but both very comfortable. In addition to my bed and dresser and wardrobe, I have an armchair near a window that looks out over the tennis courts, and a sturdy desk. After breakfast in the dining hall downstairs (airy and well laid out, if a bit noisy; over two hundred people are staying here!), we take a walk along the shore and then return to our rooms to work. We meet again downstairs for lunch and then, depending on the tide and the weather, visit the tidal pools, or take out one of the hotel's rowboats, or swim in the bathing area. The island is small (about half a mile wide, I think; and perhaps a bit longer), but so rugged and broken by the sea that we keep discovering new pools and crannies. After dinner we relax for a while on the huge porch, which stretches the length of the hotel and is lined with rocking chairs.
>
> Daphne's working furiously on a book about the plants and creatures of the shore, collecting samples (I help her with this) and comparing them with the photos and descriptions in other

books, writing up her own descriptions. I read what she writes
each day and offer suggestions, but am also working through
Darwin's book about insectivorous plants. Much of it is about
the common sundew, which grows at home, so I can easily gather
plants for my class.

Daphne knows the place already, from when she came here
alone two years ago. She also met Mrs. Thaxter, who owns the
big cottage near the hotel, then. But she hadn't really gotten
to know her, and last night she announced, with much excite-
ment, that she'd managed to get us an invitation to the evening's
gathering at Mrs. Thaxter's cottage. Apparently this is a great
coup! Only the most select of the hotel's guests are invited, writ-
ers and musicians and painters and so forth. Honestly I would
rather have had a quiet night reading or watching the stars, but
Daphne was so pleased with herself (I think she tried and failed
to get invited before) that I felt I had to go.

Some of this visit she describes in her next letter to Mason, noting especially the densely cluttered parlor. Chairs, tables, lamps,
easels, every surface covered and the walls obscured by paintings and
sketches touching each other and rising from chair rail to ceiling.
The mantels and windowsills packed with Mrs. Thaxter's famous
flowers: poppies arranged by color and tea roses in matching bowls;
sweet peas, wild cucumber, hop and morning-glory vines spilling
from suspended shells and baskets; larkspurs and lilies in tall vases
and stalks of timothy and other grasses rising above a massive vessel
with a few red poppies interspersed.

She describes the olive-green upholstery on the sofas and chairs,
the polished floor designed to enhance the sound of the piano being
played by a man in a linen jacket, the loosely draped shawls on the
women. But not the feeling she had after Daphne was pulled away

by their hostess and introduced to a circle of literary men, which closed and left her partnered with a bookshelf. The linen man played Chopin, stroked his thin brown beard and played Mozart; she studied white water lilies floating in white bowls. Daphne's face pinked with pleasure as their hostess, who was very stout, said that her book on the insect pests had been of great use to her, really *enormous* use.

Then Mrs. Thaxter rested a plump hand on Daphne's arm and ranted about the island's dreadful slugs, her bolstered, comfortably bulging self making Daphne, short and even slimmer than she'd been a dozen years ago, look like a sea oat. Where Henrietta had softened and, she would have admitted, slowed, Daphne was still furiously energetic, her small hands scored by her determined work. She nodded vigorously as Mrs. Thaxter described waging war on the slugs each morning between four and five, when the dew still lay heavy in the garden. And the grubs, the vicious grubs destroying the carnations! Mrs. Thaxter stabbed with her free hand, emulating the long pin with which she dug the grubs from the stems. Daphne suggested importing toads to eat the slugs, answered questions about the grubs, acted the part of expert regarding all aspects of insect life, which in this context Henrietta supposed she was, and yet—

Yet still it was exasperating to be so thoroughly abandoned, to see her friend showing off so flamboyantly, and to know that Daphne would never reveal to this artistic crowd that in fact she made much of her income writing cookery books under a different name. As Dorrie Bennett she had a separate and even more successful professional life, so absorbing that in the dining room she had to be careful not to draw her neighbors' attention to her judicious comments about the lobster or the biscuits. Here in Mrs. Thaxter's parlor, she might never have whipped egg whites and Cox's gelatin for her famous snow pudding, noting the time it took to raise the frothy white mass. Might never have worried over a bill or stayed up all night to meet a deadline.

At home, where Henrietta kept Daphne's cookbooks shelved next to her more serious works, she told Mason the truth about that juxtaposition when he asked: she'd wanted her two friends to understand each other. But their relationship was different now—and perhaps because of that, she hid from him her hurt feelings after that first visit, and also much about her second visit. She wrote:

> A smaller crowd last evening, four painters and a singer and a pianist, two writers from Boston, a doctor from Springfield, one of Mrs. Thaxter's brothers and one grown son (her husband passed away last year). Mrs. Thaxter sat in her gray dress next to a table covered with roses and directed the conversation and the entertainments, which included Daphne's demonstration of mounting seaweed specimens. I brought over the metal trays, filled them with seawater, stood by with the sheets as Daphne floated the samples and teased apart the finest branches with a hatpin. A beautiful piece of Cystoclonium purpurascens mounted perfectly, after which all the gentlemen wanted to try their hands. Mrs. Thaxter, as one of the younger painters observed to me, likes being surrounded by men; women are sparser, which makes Daphne even more pleased about our invitations there.

What the younger painter, whose name was Sebby Quint, actually said was more cutting than that; and he said it to Henrietta not in the parlor but outside, on the cottage's porch, beneath the shelter of the vines with their overlapping leaves. None of this, nor what followed from it, reached Mason.

IV.

*We have to do, however, in this volume, not
with the history of the past, nor with the action
of physical forces, but with the life of the present,
and to find this, in its abundance, one must go
down near the margin of the water, where the
sands are wet. There is no solitude here; the place
is teeming with living things.*

Out on the porch, where the candles cast confusing shadows, a
warm breeze pushed through the leaves encasing the columns, mut-
ing the words and music easing through the open parlor windows—
a surprisingly pleasant sensation, interrupted by footsteps behind her
and the scratch of a match being lit. The man she'd noticed while
Daphne did her hatpin trick (he was bulky, but with soft, intelligent
eyes and a way of seeming to pay real attention) lit his pipe and said,
"That dress suits you."

"Thank you," she said. She'd hoped, backing out of the room,
that no one would see her. Twice she'd tried to insert herself into the
conversation Mrs. Thaxter was orchestrating about the floating seaweeds; twice she'd been rebuffed. Bored and annoyed, she'd slipped
off for a few minutes of quiet. She smoothed the tucks of her only
good dress, glad now that Daphne had convinced her to bring it for
evening events.

"The color," he continued. "The line of the neck. You can tell it's
a success just by the way Mrs. Thaxter treats you. Your friend's in
no such danger."

"What do you mean?"

He nodded at the circle, visible through the open windows. "Dear Mrs. Thaxter likes being the queen of the hive," he said. "She doesn't always welcome attractive women."

"Me?" Henrietta laughed. For years Daphne had been chasing suitors away, while she'd only had to deal with Mason. "She must like *you*, if you flatter her like that."

"She does like me," he said quietly. "And we all like her. She makes us welcome, she admires our paintings, she sells them to her hotel guests. I'd do anything for her. But these evenings—the same people, in the same room, saying the same things, pretending rapture over the same poems and flowers . . . it's not surprising you found it tiresome."

"I was mostly hot," Henrietta protested.

"But also bored, I think. And maybe feeling a little left out? I was watching your face. Your friend was treating you like an assistant."

He puffed out a little cloud, which hung between them. Daphne, she thought, had simply been focused on impressing Mrs. Thaxter. And why was he watching her face? From the other side of the tennis courts came the clack of something hitting a rock and then a man's quick bark of laughter.

"*Do* gather," Mrs. Thaxter called. "Everyone—Donald is going to play Beethoven for us now. Everyone come!"

Henrietta turned but couldn't force herself through the door. Behind her, the painter laughed. "Where are your manners?" he said.

"Where are yours?"

"Let's be rude together," he said, after introducing himself. He brushed off a chair and waved her toward it, seizing another for himself. "Let's sit, and listen to the waves and the wind and Beethoven in the background, and relish the breeze instead of being suffocated by all the flowers and people crowded together inside. I haven't seen you here before. What's your name?"

She told him, and when he asked also told him where she lived, and how long she'd been friends with Daphne, and what they were doing there. He was from Newburyport, he said in return. A student of Appleton Brown's—"those pastels behind the row of vases are his"—kindly included in Mrs. Thaxter's invitation. He'd been sharing a small back room on the hotel's ground floor with two other students for the last three weeks. "So it's only fair I sing for my supper," he said wryly, "in exchange for a place to sleep on this fine island, three excellent meals a day, and plenty of time to paint. Some evenings Mrs. Thaxter prefers to have just her intimates; other times, if a particularly eminent guest is passing through, she'll put together a larger, more glittering group. If the guest list is more hit or miss, she'll ask me and the other students to round out the gathering and be jolly."

"Good thing Daphne doesn't know where she falls on the list," Henrietta said. He seemed to be in his late twenties: not so old that he'd object to sharing a room, but old enough to sense what that meant. Aware of how Mrs. Thaxter calculated his value. Was Daphne aware of hers?

Sebby shrugged. "Your friend's interesting enough," he said. "I can see how she'd intrigue our hostess."

"It was good of her to invite us," Henrietta said. "And I don't mean to be ungrateful. But really"—she gestured at the scene framed by the windows—"*look* at them." Three middle-aged women were gravely painting flowers in painted vases, two men were bent over an album of poems, Mrs. Thaxter herself was examining the mounted seaweed through a hand lens while a group stood around an easel watching a young man, perhaps one of Sebby's roommates, render with gold and green pastels the moon's trail on the water. All trying to convey, by their attentive expressions and postures, that they were also listening to the pianist still playing his Beethoven. All of them, including Daphne.

"You feel left out," her new acquaintance repeated.

"I do *not*," she said, more loudly than she intended. Suddenly the music stopped.

Mrs. Thaxter moved toward the nearest window. "Whatever are you doing out there?" she said, clearly affronted. "Mr. Quint, is that you?"

"My apologies," Sebby said. "I stepped out for a smoke."

"Perhaps you can step back in again, then," she said. "Or at least not disturb our musical entertainment." In the dim light, all Henrietta could see of her was a mound of white hair above, the pleats of a white scarf below. Perhaps her own features were equally erased. Mrs. Thaxter waved vaguely in her direction. "You too," she added. Did she know whom she was waving at?

SEBBY STEPPED THROUGH the parlor door, but Henrietta, disliking that sense of being summoned, left both him and Daphne behind and headed back to the hotel. She slept poorly, woke when a big storm arrived and the wind shifted and the rain began to pound, and then lay sweating in her sheets before rising to drink more than she meant to of the bottle of brandy she'd brought along for emergencies. By morning the storm had blown away, leaving the shores littered with seaweeds and all kinds of creatures—exactly, Henrietta realized when she woke, what Daphne needed. She rose and dressed hurriedly, but still she was late to breakfast and Daphne, after greeting her coolly, said very little until she'd finished her creamed eggs. Henrietta, pushing her plate aside and signaling the waitress for coffee, said, "I'll bring extra boxes this morning, and extra mounting paper."

"No need," Daphne said. "I'll manage on my own; I want to concentrate on some particular groups so I can start writing the section introductions."

"Don't be angry," Henrietta said. "I'm sorry about last night."

Daphne buttered a roll without looking at her. "There's nothing to be sorry about," she said. "You seem not to have liked it there; no reason you should. Mrs. Thaxter did ask me back this evening, though, and I'm going to go."

"I'm sorry," Henrietta repeated. If that young painter hadn't egged her on . . . why blame the painter, though, for her own feelings? "I'll behave better this time."

"Actually," Daphne said, tracing the cloth with the handle of the butter knife, "she asked if I'd mind not bringing you." The little scars netting her hands stood out in the morning light.

Beside them a large family rose, three girls in identical blue dresses watching fondly as their younger brother begged permission to go to the bathing area and their father at first resisted and then gave in. Beyond the open doors the water shimmered, the first boats were launched, the attendants opened the women's bathhouse and then the men's, a group of children ran down to the rocks and the little boy, leaping from the last of the steps, ran toward them through the rinsed soft air. What a glorious day!

"You go, then," she said to Daphne. "I can entertain myself."

"There's a concert at eight," Daphne said, pointing with her knife to the announcements on the bulletin board.

Henrietta offered again to help with the morning's collections; Daphne refused again, more firmly, and then pushed back her chair and left. Outside, the three girls in their blue dresses formed a triangle on the rocks, and Henrietta, among the last to leave the dining room, fetched Mason's hat and, after tying the muslin strips under her chin, walked in their direction and for half an hour watched the children at their sailing lessons in the cove. It was lovely, actually, to have a free day. When she went back upstairs she opened her windows wide, spread her books and papers on the desk, and settled into her own work, no hardship at all. Sailing lessons ended, bathers filled the pool, and she worked through Darwin's *Insectivorous Plants*, making notes for a set of experiments. *Drosera*, like the dew: the dew being the glistening, sticky droplets tipping the fine red hairs on the disks of the lollipop-shaped leaves. The chapters about what stimulated the hairs—tentacles, really, Darwin said—to bend and draw a possible bit of food into the cupped disk, and how the plant's secretions digested the bits, were the place to start. Each experiment offered a question posed correctly, to which an answer might be found.

Dead flies, bits of raw meat or boiled egg, specks of paper and wood and dried moss and cinders about the same weight as the flies, maybe some quills: that's all she'd need for her students to test a leaf's responses. After that, the problems weren't scientific but logistical—a huge part of teaching, as she'd slowly learned: in part from Daphne, and not just from the way she organized her scientific work. When Daphne tested recipes for her other work, substituting commonly found ingredients for tricky or uncommon ones, ordering the steps sensibly, and then scaling the result for a family dinner or a party for twenty or a wedding for eighty while working within a fixed budget, she was engaged in just the same sort of task.

They'd laughed over that many times, which Henrietta remembered when she sat down, Daphne-less, to a lunch of croquettes so nicely shaped and crisply fried, with such a savory sauce and garnish, that no one would have suspected Monday's roast turkey as their source. She ate alone, still thinking about the sequence of experiments, and then went to the lobby, where one of Mrs. Thaxter's brothers was swiftly sorting the letters and packages brought in the morning boat from Portsmouth. Among the crowd at the end of the long counter she waited for a view of her letter box: empty, nothing. Why did she feel relieved? Sebby Quint, who was right behind her and bending to view his own box, bumped into her when she turned and then continued to stand so close that she couldn't avoid talking with him.

"You disappeared last night," he said. Quite gently, almost as if he weren't doing it, he rested two fingertips on her forearm.

"I was embarrassed," she said. "Weren't you? I couldn't face going back inside the parlor."

"I'm sure it would have been fine," he said.

"I don't think so," she said, and told him about her breakfast conversation with Daphne. "Apparently," she concluded, "I'm banished."

He frowned. "I'm sure Mrs. Thaxter didn't mean that. Your friend must have misinterpreted what she said."

Only a few minutes later, when Sebby left for his easel and she returned to her desk, did she realize that she might have implied that the incidents of the night before had caused a real rift. But as brusque as Daphne had been at breakfast, she was sure Daphne's disapproval wouldn't last; they'd had worse spats and misunderstandings over the last dozen years. Often Daphne pulled away when she was first offended, only to bounce back elastically, once she'd scared herself, across the gap she'd created. The best thing was not to argue but to wait quietly for a day or two.

Henrietta ate her lunch alone twice more and both times made excuses for Daphne's absence when she ran into Sebby at the letter boxes. Daphne, she explained, working furiously on the short essays meant to introduce each phylum and class in her book, was taking her midday meal in her room.

"Busy woman," he said. He'd rolled up the sleeves of his white shirt, exposing his forearms and the little flecks of paint—carmine, cobalt, golden yellow—that dotted the tanned skin but not the burnished hairs. "Organizing the entertainments for Mrs. Thaxter's guests must take a lot of time too."

She shrugged, pretending that wasn't news. She knew Daphne continued to visit the cottage in the evenings, but they'd avoided talking about Mrs. Thaxter's gatherings during their quiet dinners together: simply, Henrietta thought, Daphne being discreet.

"The night before last, she arranged a little artificial pool and filled it with plants and creatures she'd gathered from the rock pools," he noted. "Last night"—was he summoned there every night?—"she brought more seaweeds to mount, enough so everyone could try. I sketched those, and also some of the guests. She's good at knowing what will interest people."

"She is," Henrietta said. "She's very gifted that way."

"Gifted socially, too," Sebby said. Was that admiration in his voice, or a sarcastic imitation? "She's making quite a friend of Mrs. Thaxter, and also some of her literary circle."

By the next day, when they met again, she'd begun to wonder if he timed his arrival to coincide with hers. They both had letters that day, and because he opened and read his little pile casually, at the counter, she did the same with her single envelope. A chatty, inconsequential letter from Mason: weather, news of a bicycling accident, a description of the agricultural society meeting in Ovid. *Dr. Sturtevant gave a good talk about corn, and Professor Arnold some useful notes on butter-making in winter. The best was Law on contagious diseases in animals: he talked about bacteria in a way everyone in the room could understand.* Mason—balding, friendly, freckled; just a few years older than she was—being typically Mason. He'd gone to Cornell before returning to his family farm and was interested in the structure of soil and its microorganisms. He experimented with soil amendments and, when he could find the time, good-humoredly accompanied her class on field trips. Happily busy, he never begrudged her the time she needed for her work. Both her mother and Hester had hinted that this might change when he showed up with his grandmother's opal ring—but then some other life would appear, which at least part of her had thought she wanted.

Why, then, did she crumple the pages as Sebby looked up from his own? Why tighten her lips, stare blindly at the ground, let her eyes fill? Why, when Sebby touched her elbow and said, "What's happened? Is everything all right?" turn away as if she couldn't talk? And then turn back and say, "My friend at home, Mason, the man I thought—I thought we had an understanding. But it seems he has met someone else."

Sebby drew his breath in sharply. "He's breaking off your relationship?"

She nodded.

"In a *letter*?"

She nodded again, watching sympathy and affection flood his face. He seized her hand—by now they'd stepped away from the counter—and said, "That's terrible, what can I do?"

What was she doing? Her lips were trembling, her hands as well; the story she'd invented without thinking felt almost true, and Sebby was as responsive as she'd somehow known he would be, his interest in her sharply fanned. That whiff of her needing help and leaning on him was hitting him like brandy.

"Nothing," she said. She ran a palm over both eyes.

"Nothing?"

"I don't know—maybe I could sit with you this afternoon and work on my notes while you paint? Daphne's busy and I don't want to brood by myself."

They spent the afternoon together, she in a chair drawn near the easel he'd set up on a flat rock overlooking the harbor, he moving between his canvas and her. Several times he rested his hand on her arm or her shoulder, and once she reached her hand back to rest it on his. They parted at teatime, and after Henrietta worked for a while, she answered the knock on her door to find Daphne holding a sheaf of pages, her expression cheerful and energetic.

"I did the overall introduction to the Coelenterata," she said. "And then smaller ones for the Hydrozoa, the Scyphozoa and Actinozoa, and the Ctenophora—I got so much done! Will you read them for me and see how they strike you?"

"Of course," Henrietta said: her apology, as the pages were Daphne's. She read swiftly; she took notes. She suggested several cuts and a new opening for the piece about the ctenophores. Two hours later they went down to dinner together, Daphne by then asking Henrietta about her sundews and proposing an alteration in one of the experiments. In the lobby, they ran into Sebby.

"How are you feeling?" he asked Henrietta, looking at her intently. "I meant what I said, I am so sorry—"

Daphne froze. "What happened?"

"That wretched man," Sebby said.

"Mason," Henrietta clarified. Of course Sebby assumed she'd already told Daphne—and she'd meant to right away, to confess the impulsive lie and maybe even what was driving her to pull Sebby closer: but she and Daphne had been so caught up in the relief of working together again that she hadn't had time.

"What," Daphne said now, "did Mason do?"

"To dismiss her in a letter," Sebby said indignantly. "To tell her she's been *replaced* . . ."

Daphne's face reddened as Henrietta stumbled through a quick version of the story she'd told Sebby. "What an idiot!" Daphne said. "So stolid and unoriginal and slow, so—"

They'd met several times; when she and Henrietta had visited his farm last summer, she'd spoken admiringly of his ducks and his orchard and claimed to like him. "He doesn't hold a candle to you, I never knew what you saw in him. Really, you're well shed of him."

She put her arm around Henrietta's waist. "Just like him, too, to tell you he's met someone else in a letter. Coward."

For a moment Henrietta felt properly put upon—and then, as Daphne continued to rant, amazed to learn how much her friend had disliked Mason all along. Sebby listened, made sympathetic noises, fanned Daphne's indignation. He asked if he could join them for dinner, and when Daphne encouraged him, offered his arm to Henrietta.

V.

As each wave retreats, little bubbles of air are plentiful in its wake. Underneath the sand, where each bubble rose, lives some creature. By the jet of water which spurts out of the sand, the common clam Mya arenaria reveals the secret of its abiding-place. Only the lifting of a shovelful of sand at the water's edge is needed to disclose the populous community of mollusks, worms, and crustaceans living at our feet, just out of sight.

Celia Thaxter died in 1894, nine years after the August day on which Henrietta and Daphne sailed from the island back to Portsmouth, and just a few months after she published the handsome volume about her gardens that we still read. *The other day, as I sat in the piazza which the vines shade with their broad green leaves and sweet white flowers climbing up to the eaves and over the roof, I saw the humming-birds hovering over the whole expanse of green, to and fro, and*

discovered that they were picking off and devouring the large transpar-
ent aphides scattered, I am happy to say but sparingly, over its surface . . .

That tangle of honeysuckle, hops, wild cucumber, and clematis, impossible to separate, is where Henrietta and Sebby met—but the vines are gone, and the piazza too; the hotel and Mrs. Thaxter's cottage burned down in 1914, leaving only the foundations. A marine biological laboratory occupies most of the island now. College students visit throughout the summer, studying the same creatures Daphne and Henrietta collected, sampling the tidal pools and each other. A group of ardent gardeners has rebuilt Mrs. Thaxter's garden on its original site. Hollyhocks, sunflowers, poppies, roses, the old-fashioned favorites of midsummer, which she surely would have enjoyed.

Before she died, she apparently also enjoyed Daphne's *Wonders of the Shore*. She kept copies in the hotel library, and a personal copy, inscribed by Daphne, in her parlor; she gave others as gifts to cherished visitors. The hotel declined after Mrs. Thaxter's death, as other, more modern resorts and hotels sprang up along the Maine and New Hampshire coasts, emulating and improving on the place Henrietta and Daphne knew—but all of them stocked Daphne's book for their guests. Many visitors bought copies; teachers used it in their classes. Daphne built on that success with shorter books, more richly illustrated and less technical: one specifically about the seaweeds, another about the common shells. And when she arrived once more in the village, on an August day in 1901, she brought those, as well as copies of the most recent edition of *Wonders of the Shore*, as gifts for Henrietta, her sister, and her nieces. Marion, eight and a half by then, tall and round-eyed and particularly cherished after two stillbirths, took her copy as eagerly as a girl from a different family might have taken a new doll. Caroline, who was almost five, pointed at the title and said, "I can read!" Elaine, only a few months old, kept her thoughts to herself.

Along with the books and the rest of her luggage, Daphne also brought a large flat package wrapped in brown paper, which Henrietta noticed at the train station but then forgot to ask about. They cooked and ate a simple meal in the kitchen that still, two years after Henrietta's mother's death, seemed oddly empty; they went to a meeting of the Fossil Collectors Club; they went to sleep early. The next day they had a pleasant excursion to the Grove Springs Hotel, lunch with some visitors from Elmira, and then a hectic dinner at Henrietta's sister's house. Nothing out of the ordinary— Elaine, a fussy baby, was distracted by the company and slow to nurse; Ambrose was out at a meeting; in their father's absence the older girls careened around the house as they vied for attention— but Henrietta, who came almost daily to help, was startled to see how uncomfortable this made Daphne. During earlier visits, before the baby was born, she'd been more relaxed and had even helped Henrietta put the girls to bed, but now she blushed at the sight of Hester's breast and flinched when Caroline knocked a cup from the table, a dark stream of coffee shooting from the pale china shattered on the floor.

They left immediately after the pie, and when they reached Henrietta's house, Daphne collapsed in a chair on the porch. "Sorry to be so feeble," she said apologetically. "I'm not used to that much noise anymore."

"They were excited to see you," Henrietta said, taking a seat on the glider. The wisteria she'd planted years ago had climbed the pillars and fanned across the scrollwork, filtering the glow from the streetlights through the leaves. For a few minutes they sat silently, eating cherries from a platter decorated with silvery fish, which one of Henrietta's former students had made. Then Daphne went inside and returned with the parcel, which she handed to Henrietta.

"This came last month," Daphne said, fiddling with the edge

where she'd torn the paper open. "But it was meant for you, and you should have it."

She stood with one hand on the railing. Still slight, still very erect: the resilient, resourceful person who, when Henrietta had first known her, taught herds of little boys. Her hair still golden in the leafy light and not half gray (Henrietta's by then was completely gray), and her crushed-paper skin returned to youthful smoothness.

"Do you envy your sister her life?" Daphne said. "Even when they're squabbling, they look like what everyone seems to think a family should look like. And you're so good with your nieces, it makes me wonder . . ."

Henrietta shrugged. "That's *because* they're my nieces," she said. "I'm not responsible for them all the time, just when I choose—it's easy to be good when you just dip in now and then. But no: I love those girls, but I wouldn't want Hester's life. I'm glad I avoided it."

"Me too," Daphne said. Did that mean, *I, too, am glad you avoided that life*? Or, *I'm glad I avoided that life myself*? Neither of them mentioned Mason. Daphne retreated to the room that had once been Hester's, which was where she always stayed, and Henrietta went to her own room and unpacked the parcel. First she looked at the letter addressed to Daphne.

It is not likely you will remember me, but we met some years ago on Appledore Island, where over the course of several weeks we were both welcomed into Mrs. Thaxter's parlor for her evening entertainments. I hope you will not think me vain if I say I was the painter of the watercolors you claimed to admire—Mrs. Thaxter's garden, the roses and sunflowers and so on. You were there with a friend but she came only once or twice to the evenings and I confess I can no longer recall her name. She is actually the one I am trying to find.

I was there with a friend too—one of my roommates, another painter—whose name was Sebby Quint. Sadly, he passed away earlier this year after a peculiar accident. Disposing of his few belongings has been complicated (he was estranged from his family, and never married), and as the contents of his studio passed to me I am presently trying to find homes for the work that mattered so much to him. Hence this package. There are a number of sketchbooks, but the contents date this one to the summer we all met. A few pages are of such a personal nature that I felt the entire book should go to your friend. I am hoping that you two are still in touch, and that you can convey this to her along with my best wishes and hopes that she is well.

May I just say here that I have enjoyed your Wonders of the Shore *very much, and that I remember some of what you so generously showed our motley crowd during those happy evenings? The place is, sadly, very much changed since Mrs. Thaxter's death, but I hope you too remember it fondly.*

Henrietta couldn't read the signature—a short first name, a last name beginning with a *P*? Sebby had had two roommates; she couldn't picture either one: Why should this person know about Sebby's death, when she did not? Although they'd not stayed in touch, for sixteen years he'd been as present to her imagination as Daphne, leaping to mind unexpectedly when a wave lapped at a hull with a particular sound, or a cedar branch shook off the raindrops beading up on its needles.

For a minute she tried to absorb the enormous fact of Sebby's death: hopeless. He was gone, yet the image of him in her mind remained the same, his voice still humming in her ear, his touch still warming her skin. The sketchbook, opened, smelled of him and of the sea. There were the cliffs, waves foaming through the trap dike.

Rock pools, landing dock, breakwater protecting the bathing pool from the rougher sea; within the pool, some children on a raft. Three girls dressed alike in blue, regarding a little boy. A mass of vines enfolding a porch, the vine leaves themselves, some small white flowers and twisted stems. A man—she remembered that man!—frowning intently as he drew a bow over his violin strings. A blank page and then . . .

A woman's hand, wrist, and forearm. A woman's naked back, rising in a powerful curve from the skirts heaped around it. On a ledge deeply cut into the cliffs, a woman with her face hidden by her raised arms, the rest of her exposed to the sun. A pair of woman's legs dangling over the edge of a rowboat. Did she want those to be hers, or did she not? She looked again at the penciled lines, the deft light strokes, the delicate shading. On one of the bare calves, a scar curved where hers did: her legs, then. Her arms, her back. Her self. As Sebby's friend had realized. And as Daphne must have realized too.

How little, after all, she'd kept secret from Daphne. Only the letter, perhaps; perhaps not even that.

After she lied about Mason's letter, she and Daphne had spent their evenings apart. Daphne continued to visit Mrs. Thaxter's cottage—pushing forward, she admitted, with her conquest of that circle of painters, literary men, and musicians; no one but Henrietta understood how much she depended on such connections for the success of her work. Henrietta was less frank about her pursuit of Sebby, but no less determined. When Mason's letters continued to arrive, she ostentatiously threw them out unread. She cut up Mason's hat. She pretended grief and let Sebby comfort her. She pretended confusion and let Sebby seduce her when in fact, and despite her ignorance, she seduced him. Soon he stopped going to Mrs. Thaxter's cottage, telling his friends that he was making a set of night paintings but instead spending the hours after dinner with Henrietta. On that tiny island, smaller than Henrietta's village and densely populated by summer guests and the staff who looked after them, she and Sebby still found secret spots where they curled into each other. On a pile of kapok life vests, in the corner of a boathouse. In the nooks of the northern headlands. During the day, as they worked together, Henrietta listened to Daphne disparage Mason, congratulate her for shedding him, reiterate (she herself had already shed several suitors) the enormous advantages of the single life. Then at night Henrietta undid Sebby's buttons with fingers so quick they seemed to have practiced without her knowledge.

Did Daphne know what she and Sebby were doing? Roughly, at least; probably: Henrietta had sometimes sensed (almost instantly denying this to herself) an intensity to Daphne's gaze that might have come from her sorting and weighing bits of evidence, speculating with her usual fierce intelligence as to their cause. So perhaps Daphne had known what she was doing and, since Sebby was headed soon for a studio in Rome, judged the risk acceptable—as Henrietta herself had known, without knowing the details, how intently Daphne was campaigning to win over Mrs. Thaxter's friends. The unspoken details of their night lives were, along with the work they'd returned to sharing, part of the sturdy thread that continued to bind them. Only the lie that had started it all, and the difficult scene during which, when she finally returned home, she'd broken things off with Mason, remained her secret.

She forgot it herself, sometimes: forgot what she'd done, forgot that she and not Mason had ended their relationship. She forgot, when she saw Mason and his pleasant wife and their four boys at a holiday gathering or a fair, that she'd been the one to walk away from that life—not so she could take Daphne's firm advice that remaining single was the better path (Daphne, across the hall, crackled the page of a book just enough to signal that she was awake if Henrietta wanted to talk, but busy if Henrietta needed her privacy)—not so that she could take Daphne's advice, but so that, for barely more than a week, she could touch Sebby's paint-flecked arm and feel his hair against her lips.

THE REGIMENTAL HISTORY

I. HELLO TO YOU

One of her jobs at the Deverells was to gather up the letters, after they'd been read by the family and the neighbors whose sons had been mentioned, and file them in the special box. Each envelope smoothed and flattened. Each sheet unfolded, the creases pressed out under a stack of books and then gathered and tied with clean string, laid flat with the newest letter on the top.

Henrietta was ten, almost eleven, that spring of 1863: sturdy and energetic, tall for her age, with her dark hair still hanging in two long plaits. An excellent speller with a tidy, legible hand and a curiosity that offended some of her neighbors, but not, fortunately, her new employers. Henrietta knew, because she asked, that the letter writers were Mr. Deverell's younger brothers Izzy and Vic, who were twenty-three and twenty-one, and that they'd enlisted in part because of the bounty. But what was a bounty? (Mrs. Deverell, who asked Henrietta to call her Aurie, explained.) And why were Vic's letters so short, while Izzy's went on and on? ("Brothers," Mr. Deverell said with a shrug.) She preferred Izzy's letters, both sides of five or six sheets filled with gossipy details, late additions and afterthoughts winding up the margins until he ran out of room entirely. But what was a company, what was a regiment, was a corps larger or smaller than a brigade?

"Larger," Mr. Deverell said. (He hadn't asked her to call him Maurice.) A corps was made up of several divisions, a division made of several brigades; a brigade contained four or five regiments, and a regiment like Vic and Izzy's began with ten companies of roughly a hundred men each but shrank as men got sick, deserted, were wounded, were—he stopped there, he would not say *killed*. She was taking notes.

"That," he said, as she sketched a nested set of boxes in boxes, "is enough of that. Now go help Aurie."

After the first week, Aurie gave her a pencil and let her number the pages and, if the letters were dated vaguely or sited anecdotally—*Next day, early morning. On a log, at camp 1 mi from white church*—add a tentative calendar date and location. From the newspaper Henrietta had cut out woodcuts of the camps and the hospitals. From a magazine, a map of northern Virginia showing the rivers and towns. No one minded if she read the earlier letters and tried to match newspaper accounts of events with what the letters reported, as long as she kept a close eye on Bernard.

But Bernard was an easy baby, especially compared to her own sister Hester, who was often as fretful as a newborn although she was a year older than Bernard. He was cheerful when awake and reliably sleepy at nap time, and although he was beginning to walk and had to be watched every minute, Henrietta had no trouble tending to him, helping with the housework, and then delving into the letters and papers. It was like school but even more interesting, and when Izzy described an enormous shipment of mules or the bitterns he'd seen in a swamp, she promised herself that someday she'd see similar things. Her father had taken her to different places around Crooked Lake, also a few times to Corning and Bath and twice to Rochester, once to Syracuse: but that was it. So perhaps it wasn't just the bounty, then; perhaps Izzy and Vic had enlisted last summer just to see something beyond this chunk of central New York.

Aurie said that if her husband's parents were still alive they never would have let the two brothers join up and she wished they hadn't, the pottery was impossible to run without their help. She was slight but strong, queasily pregnant, and so grateful for Henrietta's presence after school and on Saturdays that Henrietta found her tasks easy. Wash the dishes, scrape carrots, change and entertain and feed Bernard, whom Aurie claimed had weaned himself by simply refusing her breast one day, and who already ate, obligingly, oatmeal, eggs, and mashed peas. How he'd come into existence was a whole other question.

Meanwhile Henrietta ferried cups of tea as Aurie glazed bisqueware or painted underglaze decorations. She fetched and carried for Mr. Deverell as he wedged clay (a good time for questions) or (the worst time, very bad) unloaded the kiln. Twice each afternoon, a pointless task but she had to try, she swept the hall and the kitchen clear of the dust tracked in from the pottery. Then, when Bernard was napping and Aurie was painting flowers on bowls, she read and organized the letters and made lists of new questions. The notebook her father had given her was dark green, the size of a prayer book, and she carried it everywhere.

Throughout March, the letters came from the regiment's winter camp in Virginia. Izzy wrote about the other boys in their company: who had measles and who had typhoid, who'd failed to return from leave and might have deserted. Vic complained laconically about the food and the weather, but Izzy described whatever caught his eye: an observation balloon, for instance, being towed like a tethered cloud by a crew of men holding ropes. How big was *that*? Henrietta wondered. What kept it up, who invented it? Before her father's death, they'd followed the story of a balloon that had carried four men and a sturdy lifeboat from St. Louis to the northeast end of Lake Ontario, where a storm had tangled it into some trees. She envied the group of schoolgirls who'd seen the men crawl down from the branches.

It was frustrating not to be able to ask Izzy directly why this smaller balloon was forbidden to fly. One day he wrote about a general's visit, and another about the excellent meals he and his messmates made when some boxes arrived from home in which the jellied chicken hadn't spoiled, the poorly wrapped honeycomb hadn't saturated the shirts and stamps, and the dried apples hadn't grown mold. Those damp, jumbled boxes . . . Henrietta had only to look at Bernard's plate to imagine them clearly. Equally clearly, she could envision the other boys from their county who'd enlisted in different regiments and chosen to channel their words through Izzy.

Some couldn't write, Izzy said; others felt awkward writing to their families; he took requests when he visited their camps. *Levi's mother hasn't told him if the wood-lot sold. Can you find out and let me know?* This too was familiar to her. For as long as she could remember she'd helped her mother with business letters: first watching and then—she'd learned to read and write very young, perhaps from spending so much time with her mother—writing herself. The shortest form letters at first; later, letters dictated by her mother and having to do with what was left of her father's business and the patents on his inventions. A natural leap, from there, to acting as scribe for neighbors and acquaintances who didn't write so easily. She'd written letters for vineyard workers and masons, travelers and newcomers with relatives in other countries.

Aurie, when she heard about this, enlisted Henrietta to take dictation from Mr. Deverell, whose hands stiffened like an old man's from working the wheel all day. Aurie could keep painting or play with Bernard and Mr. Deverell could wrap his hands in hot flannel, if Henrietta didn't mind writing out his responses. Proud to be trusted with this task, she shaped her words carefully and saw how he softened difficult news and circled around his own problems at the pottery without actually lying. Among the letters to which she wrote a response was this, which Izzy sent in the middle of April:

Dear Maurice, This morning it is raining very hard and the wind is rattling our tent so we can hardly hear each other. Thanks for the news about Albert's sister, which cheered him. I'm glad the girl helping Aurie is working out (hello to you, if you are reading this! Your handwriting is good but you spelled "tonsillitis" wrong. Also furlough is not spelled "ferlow"). Vic has been sick with chills and fever but the doctor claims he's doing better now—good thing, as we hear rumors that we'll be moving soon. Ezra, on picket duty last week, says the rebs across the Rappahannock are buzzing about and he thinks we may be marching upriver. Two secesh boys captured; good spirits, no shoes. What news of Hinckley's arm?

"Hello to you!" An invitation, perhaps; she might ask him some things directly? Until she read his letters he'd been one of those grown boys who, like the others who'd signed up last summer, she knew only by sight: large, loud, unaware of her except as an annoyance. Now she could imagine the way he thought. She looked forward to seeing what he wrote next.

But no news came for several weeks until, at the beginning of May, a short piece in the *Crooked Lake Gazette* noted that the two armies camped all winter on opposite sides of the river had finally engaged. The following day, an article in the Rochester paper gave a clearer sense of how long the battle had lasted and how bad the fighting had been.

On May 8th, Henrietta came in after school to find a short note from Vic on the kitchen table: *I'm alive.* In the back bedroom she heard Aurie singing to Bernard, who was insisting she give him some yarn. *I have heard from several friends that Izzy was wounded, but so far I can't find him.*

Nothing else, only a line on the outside of the dirty envelope. *You must pay postage—I am out of stamps. None to be gotten here.*

She put the single sheet and its envelope directly into the letter box and then scrubbed the bean pot thoroughly. Later, when Mr. Deverell came in from the pottery to write two terse letters and a telegram, which he insisted on doing himself, she tried to help by taking Bernard out back. Aurie thanked her when she returned but said nothing about the letter, nor did they discuss it on Saturday.

On Monday and Tuesday of the following week she hardly saw either of them; Mr. Deverell was loading the kiln and needed Aurie's help, leaving Bernard entirely in Henrietta's care. She sang to him and gave him a wooden spoon and a bowl to bang while she made biscuits. On Wednesday Aurie left three letters on the table without indicating when they'd arrived or in what order. "We don't know what they mean yet," Aurie said. Pale, drawn, as distant as if she'd never hugged Henrietta. "So if you could not say anything at school, or in town—?"

"Of course," Henrietta said, setting the sheets of paper under the dictionary to flatten while she washed the floor. The first one she read came from a rebel stretcher-bearer who'd been ferrying his regiment's wounded back behind the Confederate lines.

Your brother Isidore has asked me to write this, and although we are enemies I could not deny him. I found him May 4 near a stream where many were lying hurt and all mixed together. Two Yanks who staid back when the rest ran layed your boys on the banks so ours wouldn't trample them as they advanced.

Isidore was shot twice. He fears he may die and directs me to write that he and his brother were separated but that if Rick has survived, he should have his share of the family property. I have no supplies or medicines to share with him but have done what I could to help. Will send this north with prisoners who are to be exchanged.

Next she read the one from the assistant surgeon of Vic and Izzy's regiment:

I write with the painful duty of saying that your brother Izidore Daverall is presumed dead. He was separated from his company during the rapid retreat of Friday night and while we have reports of him falling while fighting with another regiment on Saturday we can't confirm this. Since our return to camp we've been compiling our lists of the killed and wounded and I know he has not returned to the regiment; he is not to be found in our hospital; he has not been reported captured. Many were left on the field after our final retreat on Saturday. We have not been allowed to retrieve or bury our dead but fear the worst.

A third letter, almost illegible, came from Axel Weatherwax, who was in Vic and Izzy's company and whose sister Henrietta knew: he was only sixteen (he'd lied to get in) and from his writing might have been eight. His note was so hard to decipher that she wrote out what she thought it said on a separate piece of paper:

A man I know in the 123rd says he saw several wearing our Corps badge mixed in with them. All fell, either captured or dead. Vic is searching everywhere for Izzy as am I but no one knows anything.

Can you send food package for Vic? And ask my mother to send to me? Nothing here is working right. Will send more news if get some.

She had always been a good student, but that week and the next she drifted off during classes, scanted her homework, and was several times scolded by her teachers. Izzy missing, Izzy possibly dead: when she thought of how little comfort the neighbors had been when her father died, anything she could say to the Deverells seemed wrong. She'd hated the neighbors who said nothing and pretended the accident hadn't happened. Hated the undertaker, the funeral, the condolence cards and the baskets of food; hated those who probed for more details. Hated most those who assured her that her father had gone to a better place. But now she in turn was baffled. She redoubled her efforts around the house and tried to be especially cheerful with Bernard.

News arrived of the other local boys: Axel was fine, the *Gazette* reported the following week, as was Philander Scott. Ezra Mattison and Darius Tefft had been wounded. Izzy was listed among the dead. And yet one sunny afternoon near the end of May, Henrietta found Aurie and Mr. Deverell marveling over this:

Dear Brother—I'm in hospital at Aquia Creek—alive although apparently reported otherwise. A ball went through my left hand— the wound probably not too bad at first but much infected since. Was shot again trying to make my way off the field—that broke my right arm below the elbow & tore me up pretty much. Our boys scattered everywhere in the confusion of the first nights attack & caught hard words from some not there who don't know what we went through—we could not keep together & even our company was separated. That night and next morning I fought among strangers. Was overrun again—our boys skedaddled again & when

I fell was near a stream the Johnnies took. Later some moved us wounded—their enemies—to flat ground around a house. We went eight days there with no care & little food & much rain. Some drowned—I was able to sit up. Our surgeons retrieved those still alive & took us in wagons to this hospital.

Don't believe the rumors about the rout of our boys. If we ran, so did everyone—our generals did not know what to do and other regiments skedaddled too as our flank was rolled up. Vic fought elsewhere & while only grazed along the side of his head has some burns & is very shaken. It took him a long time to find me as I was not where expected, lost from corps and regiment too. Our capt. detached him for light duty a ways downriver—I must for now dictate my words & a new acquaintance has kindly volunteered.

I hope to be furloughed home when I am well enough to move—love to all & would be most grateful for news of you & any of our boys, also I need boots.

Your Izzy

(written & signed by Savery Stokes of Avoca. Yours respectfully & hello to the scribe at the other end)

He was alive; then he was dead, and then alive again. Neighbors who'd come by to offer the Deverells condolences (Henrietta retreated when they came, she took Bernard and went out back, behind the kiln and the stacks of wood, where she made him a little doll with a walnut for a head and willow twigs for limbs) left with the news of this miracle: Izzy's survival meant that not one of their own had died during what, as the weeks passed, they were told had been a terrible defeat. Everyone blamed everyone, but the corps to which their boys' regiment had been assigned came in for the harshest words of all.

So many questions—but Izzy would tell them everything when

he got home, which surely would be soon. School would end in a couple of weeks, and once she was working at the Deverells full-time she'd be able to help Aurie with whatever Izzy needed. But in early June they got, instead of Izzy in person, word of him from Vic:

Izzy's wounds are infected and the doctors are worried; he's being sent to Washington as rumored we will all begin moving north soon and the hospitals here are being emptied. I have been detailed to help with some observation balloons. At least it is something to do but I wish I was closer to where Izzy will be.

School let out and she began spending all of every weekday at the Deverells. Bernard, walking easily now, even running sometimes, had also learned to go up and down the stairs and to push open unlatched doors; Aurie had grown too big to run after him and Henrietta had to stay close to him every minute he wasn't asleep. One day she tripped while trying to catch him before he reached the heap of broken and misfired pottery behind the kiln and, as if in sympathy with Izzy and Vic, sliced open her calf. Bernard was fine, although he started to cry when he saw the blood running down her leg. He quieted only when she bound it with a handkerchief.

The lilacs bloomed and then the peonies and then the sweet woodruff; almost six weeks passed without further word from Izzy or Vic. Henrietta, the wound on her leg healed by now, built a little swing for Bernard, which he adored. The papers reported another battle, in Pennsylvania, this one a victory; a letter followed shortly after.

Dear Brother—Vic has gone missing. He is listed as a deserter—he wasn't with other soldiers returned to our regiment when Balloon Corps was disbanded, but I am sure he is someplace. If he comes home, you must tell him to come back.

*My right arm is gone below the elbow—so badly infected
it had to come off. I am being well looked after by some boys
from our company, here after the battle at Gettysburg—they say
we acquitted ourselves honorably there & suffered great losses.
When I am stronger I will be discharged & expect to see you
soon.*

Your Izzy

*(& regards from Savery Stokes. Wounded in foot at G'burg but
doing well.)*

Henrietta was eager to ask Izzy about all he'd seen and done and
felt. Instead, she felt herself pushed first quietly and then forcibly
aside. In August, during a string of days so hot that the leaves on the
trees turned upside down and the bees clustered around the spring,
Mr. Deverell sent her away when Aurie went into labor. A few days
later she returned, sure the family would need her help with the
baby, whose name was Annette, and with Izzy, who telegraphed that
he was on his way back. But three days after Mr. Deverell lifted his
brother from the wagon (she saw only the side of Izzy's dirty face
and matted hair), two days after she heard Izzy shouting from his
bedroom, Mr. Deverell met her at the kitchen door and announced
that they didn't need her anymore. Aurie, sitting at the table with
Annette at her breast, refused to meet her eyes. Mr. Deverell paid
her through the end of that week, and that was that. The family
closed in on itself so completely that by the time she started school, it
was as if she'd never worked for them. Bernard, whom she'd known
almost as intimately as she knew her sister, went back to being someone else's boy.

Had she done something wrong? No one ever told her, and Izzy,
who began showing up around town before Thanksgiving, was
always in the company of other soldiers and offered no more than a

pleasant nod when she said hello. She wasn't sure he recognized her as his brother's scribe until once, daringly, she tried greeting him with a bright "Hello to *you*!" He turned from his companion—Darius, perhaps; a big hat, pulled low, hid most of his face—and said only, "Henrietta. Yes, I know."

And then Aurie had another child, and then another. Mr. Deverell hired a man to help in the pottery but Aurie didn't hire anyone, and when Henrietta passed her on the street or saw her, surrounded by her brood, sitting on a bench near the bandstand, they talked like friendly neighbors: not like two people who had once, no matter how briefly, shared household secrets. For a while Henrietta spent too much time trying to piece together the family's new life, weaving bits of gossip she heard in town around glimpses of Izzy and the men who returned after the regiment mustered out, but eventually she forced herself to stop and she could almost feel her curiosity turning, like a stream blocked by a fallen tree, into other channels.

She had plenty to figure out: her body's preposterous changes, for one. The fact that all her friends were adults. The mysteries of Greek, which even with the pastor's help she still found difficult. She had the memory of her father and his work to ponder (his shop, behind the house, remained closed; his tools and machines had mostly been sold but a few remained, which she was teaching herself to use), as well as her own projects and investigations and the need to help her mother and Hester. How could she make some money? The royalties trickling in from a screw caliper micrometer her father had patented, which during the war had suddenly become vital to the manufacture of sheet metal, were all that kept her family afloat, and despite her mother's economies they were often short. Some girls her age did fancywork but she was clumsy with her needle and instead convinced a few neighbors to let her do boys' work. She split wood, for which she had a decided knack. Dug manure into garden plots, picked grapes, cleaned chickens. No more babysitting, after Bernard, but she wrote letters for anyone who needed a hand.

School she loved unreasonably, slicing through her studies: botany, geology, natural history in all its forms. As she moved through high school her classmates dropped out one by one, but she graduated with thirteen others and, with a scholarship and her mother's encouragement, enrolled at Oswego and started training to be a teacher herself. Mr. Williams, who'd helped her even when he couldn't quite follow her interests, retired just as she finished her training and suggested Henrietta for his job. *Reduce every subject to its elements, and present one difficulty at a time,* she learned. *Proceed step by step.*

Over the next five years, after the shock of having much of her schooling upended by her friend Daphne, she wove the ideas of the British naturalist Charles Darwin into her classes, always teaching by way of concrete examples. A dead dog, admittedly overripe, dissected by her students; a comparison of the rumen of a cow with that of a sheep. Aquariums on the benches, terrariums under the windows; seeds sprouting in low metal trays and sometimes a rescued turtle or a fledgling. Each year her students built a pair of simple microscopes and learned to use their forceps and mounted needles, examining the heads growing like flower petals from the hydras they'd slit with sharp blades. They experimented with sticklebacks, raised ants in a thin glass box, and passed around stuffed wrens and fox skeletons and the creatures floating in jars. The year that her sister, Hester, was in tenth grade, they strung together the bones of an owl she'd found, dead but almost entirely intact, in the woods. The year after that, in 1878, her class included the only other person she'd held and fed as an infant.

Bernard Deverell—what an unusual person he'd become! So peculiar, so at odds with most of the other students. So (to her) delightful. A bony boy, as slim and bendy as a horsetail. His height seemed to come from his legs; his chest was short or his waist was high or both, or perhaps that impression came from where he belted his pants. His arms, also thin, were strongly muscled and ended in huge, paddle-like hands. A crest of dark hair, never tidy, rose above his broad forehead and crooked nose. The other students might have teased him because of his boyish looks (still, at sixteen, he had only the barest bit of facial hair) or because of his obvious brilliance. Yet he was so good-humored, so wry about his disinterest in baseball and band practice and school plays, that mostly they left him to his unusual hobbies and pleasures. He was her first really gifted student, and sometimes, working with him, she had a glimpse of how she might have appeared to her own teachers.

But she'd been far more awkward at his age, far less comfortable with her own estrangement and her sense, which she'd had even as a little girl, that she wasn't going to follow the same path as most of her classmates. Bernard seemed always to have sensed that people knew he was different, and he acted as if he sympathized with the difficulties adults had in squaring his childish exterior with his powerful intellect. She had to feel her way around him, learning through his expressions that he needed mainly for her to listen to him, respond honestly to his ideas, and encourage his interests. Not just in the areas she most appreciated, heredity and evolution, botany and zoology, but in music, which he adored, and also in art and in history. Slowly she came to understand that while he loved the class field trips and laboratory demonstrations, his focus was different from hers: he wanted to study the illustrations of plants and animals and to draw his own. When he went back to his parents' pottery, he translated those images into clay. He brought her a vase he'd incised with an ichthyosaur and glazed a rich dark green. A plate on which (his class had collected frog eggs from a vernal pond) a gleaming little egg sat next to a larva, which sat next to a tadpole sprouting legs, which sat next to a finished frog. Tail, and then no tail. Limb buds, and then limbs. All the stages of metamorphosis, down to the elegant black spots. He never talked about what he did at home, what his father taught him at the pottery: but she saw, looking at these creations, how skilled he already was.

His schoolwork, his voracious reading, the pieces he made at the pottery, the music he studied with Mrs. Bagley—and something else, too, which she learned about in March. At the end of a sunny afternoon, when he'd stayed behind to help her clean up after the class had made their own batteries, he mentioned that he couldn't join the Saturday meeting of the Young Lepidopterists Club because he was helping his uncle with a project.

Izzy, he meant—who when she saw him at a concert or a wedding was courteous but no more. It was not as if they'd ever been friends; she'd barely known him when he went off to war, and since gently rebuffing her first approaches after his return, he'd treated her like any neighbor. A familiar face at the bandstand or the library, the boat dock or the butcher. If he couldn't avoid her, he'd say something about the weather, and she'd respond. Someone nearby might talk about the corn.

But if the closeness she'd felt, reading his letters, had been a girl's illusion, Bernard *was* close to him, as he let her know that afternoon. He almost never spoke about his life at home, but now, as he extracted an anode from the container of zinc sulfate solution and disconnected the wire, he explained that he was transcribing those old letters.

"Why would you do that?" A few drops fell, which she wiped away.

"Someone from his old regiment is collecting materials from the surviving soldiers, so he can put together a history. Uncle Izzy wants this man to have the letters my mother saved, but he doesn't want to send the originals. So I'm copying them over. He tells me things

while I'm working, filling in the blanks and adding more details—
it's interesting. It makes me feel like I was there. Like I can see history being made."

"I remember that feeling," she said. They'd talked before, briefly,
about her time with his family. Now she reminded him that, when
she'd been looking after him, she'd read some of the letters as they
arrived. "When your father's hands were hurting and he wanted to
write back, he'd tell me what to say and I'd write it down for him.
But you were a baby, you wouldn't remember."

"I don't," he admitted.

"And your Uncle Vic's letters—what about those?"

"There are only a few," he said, turning to the storage shelves.
"And they're all so short—Uncle Izzy thought we should set those
aside, and let Vic decide for himself if he ever gets in touch." Turning back, empty-handed, he said, "He still waits to hear from Vic, I
think. After all this time. Did you know him, too?"

"I used to see him around before the war, but I don't suppose
we ever exchanged two words. What happened to him? Around
town . . ."

"I know," Bernard said. "He's still on the books as a deserter,
and it's true he ended up in Canada. He wrote a couple times from
there, before the war ended, without ever explaining anything. Like
he was writing in code—just, you know: *I am safe and hope you are
well. Love to all.* That sort of thing. Then nothing after the end of the
war. We don't know if he's well, if he got married, if he's happy—not
even what he does for work. For Izzy, I think it was almost like he
died. We don't even have any photographs of him."

"He had an odd smile," she said, calling back a hazy image from
her childhood. "A crooked dogtooth, which I think he didn't like
to show." Probably she wouldn't recognize him now. He had vanished in a way that occasionally, caught in her own crowded life,

she envied. Even when she traveled—once or twice a year, to visit Daphne—she was always writing to her family and friends about what she'd seen. But Vic, as he'd done during the war, kept his experiences to himself. Put him at the edge of a blue-white glacier and he'd write, *Cold. Some snow.*

Whereas Izzy—still her sense of the Virginia battlefields, which she'd never seen for herself, came as much from Izzy's descriptions as from any book. *We moved through a bare country,* she remembered, *where no one seemed to have cultivated the farms for several years and pines and dwarf cedars had grown in the fields.*

They wiped down the benches and finished cleaning up. As they were putting on their coats, Bernard suggested that she come visit him and Izzy and look at the letters again.

II. IZZY

Bernard was surprised when, a few weeks later, his teacher accepted the invitation he had not wholly meant. While she often brought her students to the pottery on field trips, during which Bernard's father or his assistant patiently walked them through the steps of wedging the clay, molding or throwing the vessels, glazing them, packing the saggars and loading them into the kiln, as far as he knew she'd not been inside the house since she was dismissed. For a moment, when he heard her at the door, he saw his home through her eyes. Chairs and curtains faded, clothes and dishes and papers and toys littering every surface, so different from her orderly classroom. Skates, gloves, marbles, dolls—and presiding over all of it not his mother, who was working in the pottery and didn't come to greet Miss Atkins, but his sister Annette. A sturdy girl with round cheeks, who at fourteen outweighed Bernard and bossed their two little sisters fiercely. While she did her schoolwork at the kitchen table, Gladys and Sally played with an army of mismatched dolls. He had to force himself not to interfere when, on his way to let Miss Atkins in, he looked over Annette's shoulder and saw the problem she was working on.

If 12 tailors in 7 days can make 14 suits of clothes, how many tailors in 19 days can make clothes for a regiment of 494 men? Solve by proportion and explain. He could see the answer before he finished reading the words, but his sister—

"Does that look right?" she asked him.

"Perfect," he said, ignoring the long trail of false starts. Soon, if Annette stayed in school at all, she'd be struggling in Miss Atkins's class, where the same things that excited him—a piece of nummulitic limestone, say, and the knowledge that amoeba-like creatures had filled the connected chambers of the nummulite shells, which much later had fossilized into vast layers of stone—would make her eyes sag with boredom.

He opened the door to the person who'd taught him who he was and then stood back as she paused, just inside the threshold, scanning the room as if trying to remember how it used to look. Of the summer when she took care of him he remembered nothing. Not what his mother had looked like before Annette's birth, not the birth itself; he could remember Gladys and Sally squalling, but not Annette and not the girlish version of Miss Atkins chasing after him, as his father once claimed she had done, when he darted into the pottery and toward the kiln. The day Izzy returned from the war was lost to him too.

He steered Miss Atkins through the kitchen, funneling Gladys and Sally toward Annette. At the far end, the door that had once led to the woodshed opened now into a larger room, still a lean-to but with finished walls and a tiled floor he'd helped lay. To one side was the long couch heaped with bedding. Across from that, in a plush chair that had once been in the sitting room, sat his untidy uncle.

"Ah," Izzy said, saluting Miss Atkins ironically with the stump of his right arm. "The teacher, come to instruct us."

An hour past lunchtime, a bottle of whiskey open at his side and Izzy in a state Bernard knew well: loquacious, cheerful, nicely lubricated but not yet drunk. Often he passed his afternoons with several other soldiers in a similar state, grouped like starlings in the square. Jawing away, when the weather was fine; watching the students pour out of school when classes ended and calling out greetings to them and to the teachers, sometimes including Miss Atkins, although often she was the last to leave.

"I wanted to show her what we're doing," Bernard said. "And if you have questions about the dates—?"

On the small wooden table, within easy reach, were all the papers. He guided his teacher to the chair where Izzy usually sat and pointed out the original letters, still in the box his mother had set aside for them. Miss Atkins reached out, her fingers brushing penciled notes that—he'd known this, but in her presence finally *felt* it—were hers. His own cursive, smaller than Izzy's and neater than hers, covered the separate pile of transcriptions and the pages of additional notes.

Izzy was watching them both. In his left hand, which was frozen into a fist, the long handle of his special cup, attached at the rim but not at the bottom, arched over his bent thumb and slipped neatly into the oval between that and his curled fingers, jutting down far enough to balance the weight.

"Could you?" he asked.

Bernard, who'd designed the cup, lifted it from his uncle's hand and filled it partway from the jug of water near the window. Then, turning his back to block his teacher's view, he poured in a few ounces from the bottle at Izzy's side.

"Is it still Miss Atkins?" his uncle said. His pants, loose at the waist, held up by worn braces. His shirtfront, underneath, dotted with small holes left by his pipe, which was hard to control. A good smile, though. Wry but not bitter. "Or are you married now?"

"Still Miss Atkins," she said.

"Why is that?"

She pulled her sleeves more firmly over her wrists, as if to shield them from Izzy's frank gaze. Her dress, a color between violet and gray, had a small check probably chosen for the way it hid classroom dust and dirt; Bernard, who longed to know the answer to his uncle's question, was used to seeing her in it every other day. "I like teaching," she replied. Then, more unexpectedly, "And it's not exactly as if I have suitors banging at my door."

"No?"

"No woman my age does," she said quietly. "As you know better than most."

"We're not *all* dead," he said. "Although I suppose those left whole do get to pick and choose." To Bernard's horror he then raised his eyebrows appreciatively. "Me, I would count myself lucky."

"Look at these," Bernard said quickly.

She turned back to the letters as if she hadn't heard Izzy's comment; but Bernard knew she had. He hooked the cup into Izzy's hand and his uncle drank, and drank again, pretending he'd said nothing. No one, Bernard thought, understood why he and Izzy were close. When he was small, he'd been the only one in the family who could make Izzy smile or calm him down, even as Izzy, especially after the girls were born, was the only person who always had time for Bernard. He loved his father, who'd taught him everything about the pottery, but it was his uncle's frank affection that, before he grew so close to Miss Atkins, had made Bernard feel he could explore what truly intrigued him.

These papers, for instance. Over the pile he spread his hands, through which he'd learned so much that they seemed like extensions of his brain. Maybe because he acted so often as Izzy's hands? That Izzy let him do this easily, without resenting him, was part of what he'd wanted Miss Atkins to understand. At school, he celebrated with her the prize he won at the county fair, or the publication of the paper they'd written together about his investigations into the grape rootworm—but she knew nothing about how much he'd learned from Izzy, especially since they'd started this project with the letters. He'd wanted her to understand, although maybe not—her gaze took in everything—to watch so closely.

He shifted uncomfortably, but as he reached for the thick folder of newspaper clippings at the back of the table, she tapped his hand and said, "This is wonderful, all you've done. I'm glad you showed me—and I could check the dates if you want. Sometimes I forget how young I was when I did that."

Izzy's expression softened as he said, "That would be very helpful. Just to compare what I remember with the newspaper accounts and what you wrote down—I want to make sure everything is exactly right, since we're up against so much that is careless or just plain wrong. You'll see, if you look at these."

He batted the folder with his cup until the contents slid out.

"Fifteen years after that battle and still—why are they still blaming us? Why does our corps bear the brunt of it? Why are *we* the ones who turned, who ran, who failed to fight, who lost the battle— when everyone was at fault, the leadership failed at every level? And when many of us fought very bravely?"

He pushed at the papers as Bernard stepped aside to give him more room.

"Look," Izzy demanded. Dutifully Miss Atkins picked up first one clipping and then another. Articles, lists of casualties, reviews of books about the war. Obituaries.

"Axel Weatherwax," she said, touching one. "He wrote to Aurie and Maurice after you were wounded."

"Then he died," Izzy said. "In a different battle. The deaths are true, but so much of the rest—" He gestured with his cup and Bernard swiftly removed the handle from his clawed hand and replaced it with the fat pencil.

"Look where it says that when General Hooker testified to Congress two years later, he claimed the bad conduct of our soldiers lost him the battle. Or where General Pleasonton describes his heroic cavalry maneuvers and the clever way he reversed the cannon to batter the rebs, meanwhile watching our soldiers running away from the surprise assault of Jackson's men—an assault that a number of good men had predicted, and had warned the generals about, but to no avail. Or, or . . ."

With his pencil he pushed one magazine from the heap and instructed Bernard to read. "You know which part I mean."

Bernard read the circled passage, knowing (he knew every part of this rant) just which words Izzy would echo: *Scared sheep. Panting for breath. Bleating like infants.* Phrases that acted on Izzy like thorns.

"Why would someone make that up?" his teacher asked.

"Why does anyone lie?" Izzy said. "To make the men from other units sound better, as if they weren't running as well—there's nothing they won't say to discredit us." He bent over the table himself, elbowing Bernard aside. "Another general wrote about us that we, that we"—his voice squeaked on certain words—"*swarmed* from the woods and swept frantically over the cleared fields. And then he calls us panic-stricken hordes, a reckless crowd—he's as bad as that so-called correspondent from the *New York Herald*, reporting on things he never saw."

He looked yearningly at his empty cup. "The regiments who've already published histories remark on their own excellent behavior during the rout, claiming that while others might have run, they alone fought bravely. I'd write our regiment's history myself, if I could. But since I can't, I'm glad someone's taking the time to gather materials from all of us and write down what really happened."

"What *did* happen?" In the kitchen, something hit the floor with a crack and one of Bernard's sisters wailed.

"To me?" Izzy's left brace slid down his shoulder and he shrugged impatiently, waiting for Bernard to push it back up. "What happened to *me*, after I got separated from Vic and the rest of my company in those first minutes . . . but this is a story for another day. A story Bernard and I have to work on together, so we can send it off along with my letters, the scrapbook we're putting together of all the lying newspaper articles, which we're annotating so each lie can be addressed, and—it's a lot of work, it will take some time. And then what I send has to be collated with what everyone else sends. How he's going to find the time I don't know."

Miss Atkins, who had been following Izzy's words intently, said, "Who is it, doing all this work?"

"*You* know," Izzy said, so brusquely that Bernard wanted to groan. How would she know? She knew what everyone in town did: that his uncle drank a bit too much and repeated the same stories endlessly. She scolded her students when they made fun of that group of soldiers in the square.

"I don't," she said, a bit wearily. She pulled at her sleeves again, looking ready to leave. "But this has all been interesting, and I thank you—"

"I mean *Savery*," Izzy snapped. "Savery Stokes—he wrote some letters for me before the regiment left for Pennsylvania. You remember, when you were writing back for Maurice. We used to laugh about that, the two scribes: a big hairy soldier in Virginia, and back home this little girl. So grown-up, except when you mauled the spelling of a word."

Savery Stokes, Bernard thought. The person who, before him, had held the pen for Izzy. A person who favored the dash over all other punctuation and who always used ampersands. One brief note to the Deverells, which Bernard had since read many times, was the reason that, on a morning he couldn't remember, when Miss Atkins was still working here, his father had taken the wagon to meet the train from Bath and returned with Izzy. Remarkably thin, his father had told him later: which he also couldn't remember. With clean bandages on his stump and his remaining hand, but otherwise filthy, wearing torn clothes and a blank stare that had frightened them all. Annette had cried and only Bernard (or so his mother claimed), who'd trotted across the floor to Izzy and then tripped on his boot, had brought a smile to his face.

"Him," Miss Atkins said. "Of course. Is he a teacher too?"

Izzy shook his head. "Works for the railroad," he said. "But he does this with his spare time. He says the way to tell the real story of our regiment is to gather up as many eyewitness accounts as he can. Vic—"

To Bernard's amazement, his uncle's eyes were suddenly brimming.

"Maybe if Vic saw the history of what happened to all of us written out truthfully, he would feel like he could come home."

IZZY HIMSELF WAS killed eight years later, in an accident involving three other soldiers, a jug of whiskey, and an overturned horse cart. At the funeral, on a bright June day, Bernard plucked at the back of his good coat, through which he was gently sweating, and thought about the afternoon he'd brought Henrietta home. Those papers might convey what Izzy had really known and felt, or they might not—but now whatever he hadn't written down was gone.

Because Izzy's companions were too badly hurt to speak at the service, their company captain, a wiry little man from Bath, gave the eulogy. Flanking him along the rail were flowers arranged in four tall vases Bernard had made specially, each bearing a bas-relief of one of Izzy's favorite birds. Owl, bittern, heron, hawk. Above them bees buzzed happily while the captain reminded them all of Izzy's last battle, as if Izzy himself hadn't told them often enough. How useless the generals had been, how misguided their plans! They'd failed the valiant men at every turn. So savage had the surprise attack been that even the animals ran from the woods (turkeys, Bernard let himself imagine, and rabbits and mice, maybe one of Izzy's beloved owls), and inevitably his own company had scattered far and wide. But where a lesser man might have sought safety in the rear, or even slipped away entirely, Izzy had bravely joined the first unit he came across and, even after he was wounded, had continued to fight until a Minié ball had blown the musket from his hand.

But were there surgeons on the field to help him? There were not, nor was there a field hospital; the campaign had been so badly mismanaged that no one was in the right place and even the ambulances were on the wrong side of the river. Who was looking after the men? No one, the captain said. That Izzy and others survived after the secesh troops had passed over the field was thanks to an adjutant's clerk who'd volunteered to stay with the wounded after their own troops withdrew. He'd brought them water and fed as many as he could with what he scavenged from discarded haversacks. He stayed with them after a rebel detail arrived to move the scattered men to a central point, and he helped lay them on the ground around a ruined cabin. While the generals dithered over arrangements for a truce to retrieve the wounded, the food ran out. The rain fell and turned the ground to mud and then into a shallow lake, in which some drowned; and still the generals dithered. More died when the weather turned cold; then flies descended on the bodies when the weather warmed up.

The captain's face reddened, but despite the drama Bernard missed some of the details. If he'd spent more time with Izzy, he was thinking. If on that particular night he'd encouraged Izzy to work on his papers and share a drink with him, Izzy would not have gone off with his friends in such a bad storm, and they wouldn't have slid from the road at the top of the gorge or been dragged by the frightened horses. Instead, he'd been rushing about, constantly busy, always meaning to get to Izzy and hardly ever doing so, always with the usual excuses. His mother had died of a growth in her breast, and although his father still nominally ran the pottery, he was not himself and Bernard did almost everything now. Since his father didn't seem to care what he did, he'd slowly shifted away from making straightforward dinnerware and tiles and focused more on what excited him: ornate platters, elaborate jars and planters bearing plant and animal forms that he molded from life, casting ferns and frogs in plaster and later painting their clay counterparts to mimic their natural colors. The Durands, with their imposing house, had ordered so many platters they could fill their holiday table; a banker in Syracuse bought several planters each year; he had a dealer in Rochester and another in New York. How lucky he'd been to find a market! Especially when he was so happy designing and making them or talking with his old teacher—he called her Henrietta, now—about what he might make next.

He longed to move back a few pews to where she was sitting. The ten years between them, a lifetime when he was a schoolboy, by now hardly mattered. She'd always ignored it and had taught him to do the same, introducing him to her friends as an equal. He'd met Daphne Bannister, who lived in Massachusetts but visited. Mason Perrotte, a farmer he otherwise wouldn't have gotten to know, with whom she'd spent a lot of time until they suddenly stopped keeping company. Mason himself had come to the service, sitting below the east window with his new wife, visibly pregnant and as freckled as he was, a woman who—what was the captain saying? Something about Izzy's loyalty to their regiment—seemed to be the reason Mason was no longer Henrietta's friend. What speckled children they would have.

The captain said something bitter about how Izzy's loyalty was even more remarkable, given that the rest of them had been forced across the river, far from those they'd left behind, sent there against their will by the same commanders who declared Izzy dead even as he struggled during those days. And then there were still more words, and then prayers, and the trip to the cemetery, and the gathering back at the house, where Annette had done her best to help their father organize a proper meal. By the end of the day Bernard felt as though they'd buried not only his uncle but all his painful recollections of the war and his own inadequate attempts to help Izzy commit them to paper. A relief, at first, to put all that behind him. With Izzy gone, the arguments about statues and memorials and the fading memories of generals now running for office didn't mean so much.

For two months he put off the task of cleaning out Izzy's squalid room, finally tackling it on a day when his sisters were off at a church picnic. Under the armchair, among the dried tobacco shreds and flies, he found a four-page printed circular with fancy type and headlines, which he vaguely remembered arriving a few years ago.

The regimental history was finally underway, the pages claimed. The compiler and editor, S. Stokes, was seeking a publisher even as documents continued to accrue; letters, relics, memorabilia of all kinds might be sent c/o the Avoca Town Library and would be received gratefully. Testimonials from those who'd already contributed letters and reminiscences urged others to do the same so that the work could be finished and they could see their story in print. Fine, he thought. Let that person, whose name he still remembered, do something with the relics of Izzy's war. He packed up the remaining letters and scrapbooks and sent off two boxes.

He got no receipt in return, no acknowledgment at all. He worried about this and then, in the press of work at the pottery and his family's demands, forgot it. Also he met a girl named Mary, who intrigued him. Nothing came of that—she married a newspaperman from Rochester—but the following year a letter came for Izzy, which he opened.

October 13, 1887

Dear Mr. Deverell—

Please forgive me for intruding on you. I have taken on the duty of writing a history of my regiment and I am seeking news of your brother, whom I knew as "Vic." Our regiment was raised in Washington County in August of 1862, drilled and trained at Arlington Heights before heading to Harpers Ferry for guard duty and then going into winter quarters first near Fairfax and then, after the mud march, into the cabins abandoned at Stafford. During the battles that May our paths may have crossed. On the evening of May 2, after heavy fighting was noticed to our right, portions of our Corps were rushed to the valley and across the open field. There we crossed great numbers of men from your Corps, in forced retreat after you were flanked. The men were moving with utmost haste, jackets and knapsacks and caps flying from their hands, even their guns in some cases, regiments all jumbled together and pouring through our line as we braced to fight. We lost 10 men there, nothing compared to what you saw but hard enough. You and your brother might already have been separated from each other and the rest of your regiment by then.

After the 12th we were encamped on the other side of the river, near the courthouse, through the rest of May and June. Half a dozen of us were sent on detached duty to the Balloon Corps, where we served as ground crew, repaired the netting and so forth. Some Massachusetts men were with us and also a few from your regiment, including Vic. He proved his worth quickly, helping to rig a temporary gas generator after a storm that destroyed four barrels of iron trimmings and several carboys of acid and damaged the field generator. When another heavy storm came up during a later ascent and caused a weakened seam to explode, he helped lower balloon and aeronaut to the ground. The director appreciated his skill and asked to retain him for another few weeks when your regiment requested the return of its men.

Some confusion resulted from this, and your colonel apparently reported him as a deserter when he didn't return with the others. I was back with my own regiment by the time the work of the balloonists was terminated and assumed he returned to you then, but later heard he could not be found before the march that ended at Gettysburg, nor after. I have no record of his whereabouts since.

Because we in our regiment found our work with the aeronauts so interesting, and because Vic played a role before the Balloon Corps was disbanded, we would like to include in our regimental history some mention of his life after that time. We all wondered if the nightmares stopped and if his ability to eat *returned. All he would ever tell me about his injuries was that he was knocked unconscious by a bullet grazing his head and was still there on the morning of May 4 when the Johnnies came through to bury those who'd been lying there wounded since the day before and then trapped when the shells lit the woods on fire. The heat from the fire had waked him and he was able to crawl away but said most were not so lucky and that he saw the rebs rolling the roasted bodies, trying to determine from bits of uniform which army they'd fought with. I still remember him crying when he told me about the scraped dirt around some of the bodies, where the men who'd been alive when the fire started tried to push the leaves and twigs away from themselves.*

How Vic got so far from your regiment I do not know. Nor do I know how he eventually found you, or if he saw you again when he finally left the aeronauts. Whoever approved the Balloon Corps' request to keep Vic those extra weeks must have been lost in the battle. I can find no paperwork related to his assignment. If you would be able to put us in touch with him, or tell us anything about his fate since the war—I and my fellow veterans would be most grateful. I write this as a private citizen, but the bank in Troy where I have worked these fifteen years supports my efforts and you may send any response or supporting documents to my office here.

And there it was, a glimpse of Vic's story, but sent too late to be of comfort to Izzy and still missing answers to the most important questions. Izzy had sometimes worried that Vic had fled even before the battle at Gettysburg; other times that, if he'd fought there, he'd been wounded again, perhaps even more severely—but the man from Troy seemed to know nothing about that, never mind that he'd landed in Canada. Still—how could it be that he was so far along with his own regiment's history that he could reach out for news about men like Vic, who'd been only tangentially attached to it, while the history of Izzy and Vic's own regiment remained an utter blank?

Their own self-appointed historian had, still, published nothing but those teasing circulars. Meanwhile a long series of articles and reminiscences had appeared in the *Century Magazine*, which everyone read: many written by generals describing their battles, each concerned to amplify and glorify himself and his men. In their wake, so many letters poured in from readers, furiously complicating, contradicting, complaining, that the magazine had added a new section for them and the letters those engendered. Long-ago battles were fought once more, the smallest details disputed violently. Twice, despite swearing he wouldn't be drawn in, Bernard called on Izzy's stories to write letters of his own.

When those weren't published, he began to wonder how many others also hadn't been published. And then about the letters that couldn't be written, because the people who might correct a lie or revise a wrong supposition were no longer alive. And then about the publisher's decision to gather those articles into fat volumes that sold very well—their own library had bought the whole series—but included none of the letters originally printed in the magazine, obliterating that supplementary history. Which shed a different light on what this man from Troy was doing—

"Just read it," Bernard said, handing Henrietta the letter after explaining some of this. They were in Henrietta's room at the high school again—her classes were large that year, and the benches in the back were uncomfortably crowded—and in the clear north light of the large windows she looked a good deal older than when she'd taught him. The terrarium behind her held clusters of sundews, which he hoped to model, complete with the clear drops at the top of the reddish hairs and a fly caught in its sticky trap. She read the letter dutifully; then read it again with more interest. "*What* fire?" she said.

"What fire indeed?" he said. "Izzy never mentioned any such thing." The page showed not a single strike-through or hesitation. Copied out, most likely, after one or several drafts.

"Do you think Izzy knew much of the rest?"

Bernard had struggled to piece together comments Izzy had made over the years, always in different contexts, never related to each other. Especially after Aurie's death, Izzy had had spells when he drank so heavily that he no longer made sense even to Bernard, and Annette had had to keep their younger sisters out of his way. "Some, I guess," he said. "He knew Vic was working with the Balloon Corps for a few weeks—I remember him mentioning that. Maybe he knew that Vic had been asked to stay on. He told me a story once, when he'd had a lot to drink, about Vic being up in a balloon himself—over Falmouth, I think. Or maybe it was someplace else, in the mountains—"

"Vic went *up*?"

"It doesn't seem very likely, does it?" Bernard admitted. "Now that I say that out loud. But I swear, I remember him telling a story about Vic in a balloon with another man, hitting a patch of cold air—maybe this was during a thunderstorm? And how snow began to fall on their heads, dropping into the basket from inside the balloon. Izzy kept asking how that could happen. He'd been drinking all day, and somehow it was the snow that seemed to bother him more than the idea of his brother floating around."

"Wouldn't that be dew?" Henrietta said. She fluttered the fingers of her left hand in vertical trails. "If it condensed inside the balloon, and then suddenly froze, it would fall as sleet, or even snow."

"That's just what I told him," Bernard said, struck again by how similarly their minds worked. "He called me an idiot."

Henrietta frowned and slid the letter from Troy back into its envelope.

"Maybe he was just imagining that Vic went up," Bernard continued, "because Vic so badly wanted to do that. Or because Izzy himself did."

"Maybe," she said doubtfully.

Izzy had cried in his sleep. On rainy days, when his frozen hand twitched with pain, he'd burrowed into his blankets like an animal. The books he pored over, the games he played with Gladys and Sally; the times when, after the girls were in bed, he joined Maurice in the sitting room and talked about Vic and their childhood—how could Henrietta, who knew none of this, understand the way that Izzy thought? Her mind, Bernard imagined, was as neatly ordered as this room, which he normally loved but which today annoyed him. On a clean white shelf, above the mounted skeletons, she'd arranged a series of books her friend Daphne had written for children about the seashore, the forest, the open fields. Even Annette had been able to follow the diagrams in the one Henrietta loaned her.

"What's the *point* of those?" he said abruptly. "What's the use of oversimplifying the world like that?"

"We don't learn everything at once," she said. "You might have liked those yourself, when you were eight or ten—you just don't remember what it was like knowing nothing."

Without quite meaning to, he rolled his eyes.

"And you're not a woman," she added, more tartly, "trying to make a living solely by your pen. Daphne's not too proud to seek an audience."

"Ehh," he said. "I'm sorry. Just ignore me." All the things she'd taught him—the Guyot's maps behind her, with the countries colored and the mountains and oceans delineated sharply, were marked all over with her own notes, showing what trees grew here, what fossils were buried there. "I'm feeling guilty about Izzy. Now I wish I hadn't sent those papers off, since his friend in Avoca doesn't seem to be doing anything with them. I might as well have saved them for this man in Troy."

Henrietta turned away from him and, with a pair of long, slim tongs—where did she get those?—plucked a glistening sundew from its spot in the terrarium and moved it to the other side.

III.   THE OTHER SCRIBE

On the stone steps in front of the library her grandfather had built, where by virtue of that connection she'd been allowed to continue her brother's work, she'd been sitting with her skirt stretched wide, trying after all the rain—the limestone walls held the chill for days—to warm herself in the afternoon sun before returning to her desk. Suddenly a cool shadow; suddenly two strangers. The woman in her late thirties, around Sissy's own age; the man—odd-looking, spindly but with bulging forearms and large knotted hands—in his mid- or late twenties; the two clearly bound, but not in a way that seemed romantic. Friends, then, but unusually close. And both of them prickly, almost suspicious, expecting—what? Her brother, a book, an organization, a printing press? Not, obviously, her. Since they couldn't be allowed into the room in that state, she'd brought them out back, behind the library, where they could get used to her and where she could organize her thoughts.

Past the two curved stone benches, down the overgrown flagstone path that wound past the birdbath and the pinkly flowering hedge, roundaboutly to the pleasant distractions of the chestnut grove. As these newest strangers had come from the village on Crooked Lake (she imagined the steep hills, the rows of trained vines, the grapes hanging clumpily), she thought Mr. Demario's efforts might appeal. Half the grove coppiced, the thick stumps crowned by healthy straight shoots cropped every third year for vineyard stakes and trellises; half left to grow for timber, those trunks enormous and solid and the ground between them dense with fallen burrs and leaves. She'd known this stand of trees all her life, and as her head began to clear, she thought—but one of the strangers was eyeing her curiously, ignoring the trees and the enormous clouds rolling sheepishly through the sky.

"What a nice place!" said the other: Miss Atkins, sniffing a long, toothed leaf and admiring the exuberant flame-colored fungus sprouting from a stump. A high school teacher, her companion had announced. And an accomplished naturalist, expert in everything to do with birds and fish and rocks and trees. He himself was Bernard Deverell, nephew of two soldiers from the local regiment, looking for the Savery Stokes who'd been gathering materials for a regimental history. On the steps, he'd held out a grubby circular and asked, as stiffly as someone twice his age, to whom he had the honor of speaking.

"Sissy," she'd replied, knowing her married name would prove confusing. Other parts of this awkward encounter had also occurred before. Hence the walk out back, the viewing of the grove, the further distractions of the hogs munching last year's mast on the other side of the fence. "The present S. Stokes. My brother was Savery."

While the hogs snuffled and grunted with pleasure, while the clouds moved and the wind blew, the conversation occurred during which they, like the visitors who'd come before them, absorbed the news that Savery had died four years ago and that she'd taken over his project. Miss Atkins murmured how much she'd been looking forward to meeting him, while Bernard seemed more upset by her failure to announce this earlier than by her brother's actual death.

As the woman pretended to inspect another of the coppiced trees, Bernard, studying a bracket fungus, a lady's slipper, the elongated ellipse of a woodpecker's nest, bit back whatever he really wanted to ask and said, instead, that they'd be grateful to see what her brother had collected. She nodded and turned back down the path. The library's rear door, still unlocked, opened easily. The pair followed her past the wrought-iron shelves and the volumes carefully arranged by the librarian, Mrs. Holmes, who, in return for Sissy never touching the books in the main room, never, ever, touched Sissy's papers.

"I meant to come earlier," Bernard said. "I thought about it in '83, when there were all the gatherings marking the twentieth anniversary of the battle where my uncle Izzy—Isidore—was wounded. Then again in '86, after he died. I sent the last of his papers here, because he so much wanted to contribute to some record of what had happened, and I thought—"

That first name leapt forward, as the last name had not, from the great file of names in her mind. Isidore whose arm had been lost; Izzy of the unexpected gift. Not from Savery's company, not even one of his special friends, despite the bond they'd shared for a few months during the summer of 1863. Here, as if she'd summoned him, was his young relative.

There were two sets of papers, Bernard was explaining: as if she hadn't figured that out. This compact storeroom, where she'd carried on with Savery's work when no one else was interested, held crates once packed with wine or teacups or cheese, now stuffed with letters and scrapbooks, photographs and newspaper clippings, the bounty men from the regiment had sent in response to the circulars Savery had distributed throughout the state. Their scraps and relics had filled his barn. Swords, hats, buttons, badges, stained cockades and torn memorandum books; he kept whatever they gave him, although organizing it all—she could admit this now—had been beyond him.

"The first set my uncle sent some time back," Bernard said. "The others I packed up and sent myself, not quite two years ago. I should have checked before sending those on. If I'd known about your brother . . ."

Savery, with his left-leaning limp and his spiky dry hair, who when she was small had made dolls for her out of corn husks and who, after the war, had settled into the desk job a neighbor was good enough to offer. Before the war, he'd wanted to go to the Colorado Territory and search for gold. Now Colorado was a state and he, like Izzy—

"My brother left three children," she said, "and a wife—I'm sure you understand. And I have two daughters of my own. There was so much to do that for a while I just set the papers and letters aside when they kept arriving. But then the library director kindly offered this storeroom, and as soon as I could I brought the papers here and started work on the project myself."

As she spoke—she had given this speech before—she watched Bernard's companion ease her way into the room. Looking, judging. Scanning the dusty mounds. The school bell sounded across the square, a cardinal called, the fat white cloud to the west of the grove drifted east and shadowed the window, so deeply surrounded by shelves and boxes that it looked like a porthole. She'd grow tired, Sissy thought. They both would. The papers would baffle them and they'd leave. Visitors came at inconvenient times and almost always interrupted some vital chain of thought, but then always left.

She'd had widows visit, grown children, a few elderly parents. One or two sisters, but not, until now, a nephew. Certainly not one who brought along his former high school teacher, who at this moment was feeling her way along the high ridge of open crates along the north wall, moving so quickly and decisively that she might have been a girl. A little worn, a little tired, but still slim and brisk, less like Sissy herself than like her own tall daughters, Joan, at eighteen, about to marry, and Clare, almost grown at sixteen. They had their father's height and narrow build and couldn't imagine, when they helped her into her capacious corset or repaired a gusset torn by her thick arms, that once she hadn't looked so different from them. Hips, thighs, stomach—those slabs of flesh enclosing her now, leaving nothing untouched but her narrow wrists and ankles, had only begun to form when she was carrying Joan. Beneath the flesh that had accumulated through the sheer work of tending to them and her husband, Savery's wife and children, their bills and farms and needs and injuries and illnesses—her real self had disappeared.

Then she'd inherited this project—and everything changed again. For whole days she sat in this room, absorbing all Savery had so patiently gathered and adding the scraps that continued to trickle in. Reading, making notes, drawing up plans and outlines; seldom actually writing but thinking, thinking, about what she *would* write—it made her feel that she too had been coppiced, her old thick self cut down to a clean stump, free to sprout fresh green wands.

"Would you have an outline?" the teacher asked. "A table of contents, perhaps? Your brother might have made some maps . . . ?"

As if those were for others to see. They were foundation, underpinnings, materials she'd draw on for the sturdy quilt that would in time surprise them all. Instead she offered the copies Izzy had sent to Savery in 1880, which were in a crate that had once held oranges. No, two crates—and they were behind the stack holding the letters saved by the young wife of the adjutant killed in '64, and the brown hatbox sent by the officer who'd been college chaplain to three boys who'd enlisted together . . .

The room was so small that other crates had to be pulled out carefully, restacked and rearranged until finally—she asked her visitors to help—they reached the old orange crate and its companion, which had once held red wine. These she had Bernard balance on the corner of her working table. He reached for the sheaf of paper that lay on top, dusty and dotted with what she wished were bits of bark or leaves but were more likely mouse droppings.

"These are the ones," Bernard confirmed. "The ones I transcribed when I was in high school." No acknowledgment of what she had done, Sissy thought. No word of thanks, although without her, Savery's wife would have burned everything he'd left behind.

"I remember seeing the originals," Miss Atkins said, bending over the pages. "When I was a girl." She reached out but then politely turned to Sissy, who had preserved them. "May I look?"

"Of course," Sissy said. The teacher read a few pages, doubled back and seemed to read some lines again; put her hand to the tidy braid coiled at the back of her head. Sissy, reflexively smoothing her own faded frizz, said, "What is it?"

"Just—" Her gaze slid from Sissy to Bernard. "I thought I remembered these very well, but Izzy plays more of a role than I thought, and has more opinions about the generals' orders. And here, where he talks about Vic and his work with the observation balloons—I didn't think Izzy knew much about that. I hate to see that I've forgotten what he wrote."

"Really," Bernard said, turning toward her, "I don't think you misremember much."

"It's a long time ago," she said, shaking her head. "But still—I thought I was paying better attention."

Bernard picked at the loose paint on Sissy's chair, letting flakes fall to the floor while Sissy's thoughts rearranged themselves. *The originals*, Miss Atkins had said. *I thought I remembered.* This middle-aged schoolteacher who stood so erectly, whose skirt betrayed deep and unladylike pockets inserted along the seams—the corner of a notebook peeped from one—and who seemed not quite to notice her, must once have been the girl who had sometimes held the pen for Izzy's brother.

"I might have—I did—change a few things, when I was transcribing them," Bernard said. "To make a better story, to make Izzy feel better; and maybe so that when the history was published Vic would feel like he could come home. I didn't know the book wouldn't get written."

"Yet," Sissy protested. Savery had never been able to track Vic down in Canada, although he'd been mentioned in the letters of several men from the regiment. "It's not written *yet*. My brother didn't *choose* to die."

Miss Atkins, still ignoring Sissy, traced the parentheses dotting the pages like fallen eyelashes. "You mean these?" she asked Bernard.

"Corrections," he admitted—causing the little mechanism in Sissy, which weighed and measured the content of various letters, to spring up alertly. She'd assumed that the many parenthetical phrases reflected the habits of Izzy's mind (his hesitations, his qualifications), just as Savery's frequent dashes and ampersands expressed his vibrant haste.

"Amendments," Bernard continued. "Things that Izzy said he forgot to mention when he was writing. He had me add those in as I was transcribing each letter, but since what he added was sometimes a little different from what he'd written fifteen years earlier, I put the new parts in parentheses, so we could tell which words were written when."

"That," Sissy said, "is something you really should have told Savery."

"Or me," Miss Atkins added, looking as hurt as if Bernard had failed to invite her to a birthday party.

"You were only there that once," Bernard said. "You never saw us actually working together."

"Did you ask me back?" she said, the answer evident in her tone. Almost Sissy could see the girl beneath the seamless bark she'd grown.

"Did you ask to *come* back?" When Bernard swallowed nervously, Sissy saw that the skin on his throat was smooth and fair and that he was younger than she'd first thought. "Or ever ask more than politely about Izzy, or how my work with him was going?"

"I didn't want to pry," Miss Atkins said. Again Sissy wondered about the nature of their friendship. "I thought Izzy—maybe you too—wanted to keep some of that private. What Izzy was going through, I mean. When he first came back, your parents dismissed me with no warning at all, and I thought that was Izzy's doing. That he didn't want to feel like a stranger was looking at him."

"I can't remember," Bernard said. One huge hand wrapped around the other, knuckles bulging. "But," he added hesitantly, "more likely it was my father. He didn't tell me until after my mother died how furious he was to have been left behind to tend the business while his brothers went off to war. And I do remember him and Izzy fighting. About Izzy's drinking, and his friends, and the fact that my father had to support us all—maybe that's what they didn't want you to see."

The letters they were talking about, which Savery had kept (which she had saved) were right here. To Bernard, Sissy said, "At least you made those changes sensibly—now we can reconstruct what your uncle wrote at the time, when he was experiencing it, and what he said or thought ten or fifteen years later, after he'd heard the stories of others, and read other accounts, and had time to think about it all. Also we can compare the copies with the originals."

"Which you must have," said Bernard. "I couldn't bear to look at them again, but I know I packed them." He touched Sissy's shoulder lightly, urgently. "Two brown boxes, sent here the August before last—they're here?"

"Somewhere," she replied.

Clearly he'd never thought about what they might mean to her. She'd let the boxes sit for six months, among a pile brought from Horseheads. Then found, as she finally began reading and sorting the letters, several written in Savery's youthful hand. She had mountains of pages he'd left behind more recently, but the image arising from Bernard's accidental gift—the young Savery of twenty-five years ago, with a board on his knees and a pen in his hand, taking down the words of his companion—had made her burst into tears.

"Not in those boxes, though," she said. "And not in the same order you packed them. I have a new system these days. When I get fresh materials I put things relating to one battle with everything else having to do with that battle, and material related to one general or one incident with material others have sent related to that incident or general or battle. That way, when I start writing, I can instantly put my hand on all the different versions."

Miss Atkins, who'd been silent since Bernard mentioned his father, drew a deep breath. "When you *start* writing?"

"Those alterations," Sissy continued, ignoring the intrusion. "If I'd known, when I first looked at the papers you sent to Savery—"

She took a page from the folder of Bernard's transcriptions. *Our boys scattered everywhere in the confusion of the first nights attack & caught hard words from some not there who don't know what we went through—(our generals gave us such poor information and contradictory orders that) we could not keep together & even our company was separated.*

Now that he'd told her, she could see it: two minds at work. Or one mind at two different times; or, looked at another way, three minds if Savery had altered anything as he first wrote down Izzy's words. That was interesting, it might change the final account.

"But the scrapbook," Bernard said, pulling from the wine crate a volume Sissy had looked through many times. "The comments scribbled in the margins of the newspaper articles: Izzy did write those. At least I think he did, the notes aren't mine."

"I'll use that," Sissy said. "I use everything, to keep the stories straight."

Before Savery died, he'd once said that even a person like him who'd been *in* the war, part of the war, would after a few years no longer be sure which events he actually remembered and which he'd been told about by someone else—Izzy, for example—who'd also been there. They saw the same thing, but not the same thing. They felt the same things, but not the same things—and in talking to each other, both right after the various battles and movements and then as they retold those events, sometimes in the company of others and always with liquor involved, all the stories tangled together. Which strand came from him, which from someone else? Even he had not been able to remember sometimes—and if that was true for Savery, then she could do no worse and might even do better. Exactly because she hadn't been there, she thought, she had the chance to separate out from the strands of evidence what was legend and what was not. Maybe she could see, as those who'd been present sometimes couldn't, how one place had been conflated with another, two wings of a battle fused into one, how time had been compressed or expanded.

She'd started a number of sketches, including one she wouldn't show this pair: a little scrap about Bernard's uncle, which had arisen from that glimpse of her brother writing out the wounded Izzy's words, sending his own greeting to Izzy's brother and the girl who sometimes held that brother's pen. A little sketch, nothing yet. In time it would fall into place. A soldier from Troy, a fellow amateur historian who'd received one of Savery's early circulars, had sent in February a history of his own regiment that referred to a few men from Savery's regiment. With that, added to all she already had, she hoped to weave the story of the battle in which Izzy had been injured.

Bernard, clutching the scrapbook as well as the folder of transcribed letters, said, "I think I should take these. If you'll forgive me—"

He was trying, Sissy saw, to make the scrapbook less visible behind the folder, which he'd squeezed almost flat. As if she didn't have other copies; as if others from their regiment hadn't sent the same clippings with their own marginal annotations. Anyway, the originals (Savery's comments; Savery's sprightly dashes) were here if she needed them. That she could not lay her hand on them, just now, meant nothing. Somewhere they existed, and also many others— letters sent to her by men who knew the Deverell brothers, and those who did not, those who had been there at the worst moments of the battle and the rout and those who'd been elsewhere; those who'd seen the carnage and the fire and the balloon that watched them all from above. Some were vivid, some were dull; some were boastful and some were silly and some were straightforward and sounded honest. She would write when she was ready, when all the notes had been collated and all the versions brought together.

"Take those, if you want," Sissy said kindly. "They're your family's, after all."

"We'd leave them here, if you were going to finish the book," Miss Atkins said—then stopped, her face filled with questions, her excellent manners seeming to struggle with her curiosity. One hand toyed with the notebook in her pocket.

"If," she said. "When—" And then, reluctantly, "I could—I do know how hard you must work. My dear friend writes natural history books, and it's always a struggle for her both to find the time to do the work, and then to actually do it. She's very meticulous and

I can see you are too, you must have had your own difficulties. I've
written some things myself, so—"

"Books?"

"Articles, mainly," Miss Atkins said. Not about people, Sissy
gathered. Moths, mosses, trees. Not about what people did. Bernard
said, "We've written some together," but still Sissy pitied her. Why
study a tree when you could study a person?

"*My* book will get done," Sissy said calmly. "I don't need those
papers to do it."

"But," Bernard said, "if you're to include my uncles—"

"I know what they did," she said. In her notes she could track
the hours when the enemy had crossed unseen past their front
and flanked them, the hours when the entire corps, including this
regiment, had thought itself safe and taken a rest, prepared some
food. The hours of the rout, the slaughter, the disintegration; the
hours of separation and chaos; the hours of terror and then the
days afterwards. Because she could not trace Vic's fate directly,
she'd decided, not to erase him from the record, since there was
no record, but to pleat his experiences in with his brother's, in that
way preserving at least some of what he did and felt. After tunnel-
ing through her notes many times, she thought she'd found a way
to combine the two brothers' experiences so that in her version,
when she wrote it, a single Deverell would have been shot three
times, a ball through each arm and a third grazing his head, which
had left him lying among the dead in a copse that had caught fire
when it was shelled, burning so fiercely the men had burned too,
leaving Deverell and several companions to be pulled aside and
later brought to a low-lying cabin where the ground on which they
lay unattended had been flooded by the rain.

As the men, who came from this regiment and others, lay waiting for rescue, a huge balloon would rise to the east, and although

the observer inside would be invisible (she had to imagine this carefully, as the wind had been too strong those days for an actual balloon to have actually risen: but some men claimed they remembered one), the men lying there, burned and wounded and wet, would be comforted by the knowledge that one person at least knew what they were going through. Down the tethering line would slide a note enclosed in a little capsule that, when it made its way to the officer waiting for it on the ground, to the general back across the river, perhaps finally to the president himself, would make their story clear.

꙲

HENRIETTA AND HER MOTHS

FOR A CLUB GATHERING LATE IN THE SPRING, HENRI-
etta chose rosy maple moths, which Marion loved. A moth like a
flower, a moth like a doll: the body furred in soft yellow, legs and
feathered antennae bright pink, dark eyes shiny above pink and yellow wings. She had some pupae just ready to open and the afternoon's program planned, before discovering she'd have with her not
only Marion but also her two other nieces.

Elaine she could cradle, tightly wrapped, in the crook of her left
arm, freeing her right hand to handle specimens and write. Marion
could sit at the worktable with the four young lepidopterists cur-
rently in the club, but Caroline—how hard it was to keep track of
her! She sat at the table, knocked a jar over, jumped up and rummaged through the bookshelves, sat again and watched Sadie wield
a small brush, accidentally crushed a chrysalis, burst into tears—she
was five, Henrietta reminded herself as she jiggled Elaine; still five, a
little girl—and was consoled only when Henrietta pulled out a special low chair she favored and set a screen partway around it, making
Caroline a private corner.

"If you could help me," Henrietta said, "I want to put you in
charge of your sister. *You*," she said firmly, depositing Elaine into the
same calico-lined wooden box where Marion had once napped. "No
one else. It's a lot of responsibility but—"

"I can do it," Caroline said, leaning protectively over the box. "Just me."

WHEN HENRIETTA WAS small, she'd loved the small square building behind the house: the workshop where her father dreamed up mechanical devices and built the patent models he sent off to Washington. A trickle of income from his most successful inventions still, years after his death, kept the family afloat. A few years after Henrietta started teaching at the high school, she decided that she'd work there just as he had—what could be more natural? Once she'd cleared it out, polished the windows and repainted the floor, it didn't need much else. A coal stove, a sink, some shelves; she paid a handyman to install those. Then, delighted with the result, she moved in most of her specimens. Lovely, said her mother, who often complained of the clutter in the house. Perfect, she said, when Henrietta further transformed the building into an insect nursery.

Although really, Henrietta thought, her mother *had* to defend it. Otherwise she might have seemed to be criticizing her daughter. The neighbors called it "the caterpillar room," and while a few were charmed, others stopped crossing the backyard and Mrs. Weatherwax avoided the house entirely. Let them fuss, said Henrietta's mother calmly. She showed curious visitors how the marvels inside were arranged. Caterpillars, chrysalides, cocoons, and eggs; breeding cages and glass jars filled with green branches; winged adults drinking from sugar water–sprinkled moss and everything neatly labeled: *White-Lined Morning Sphinx. Hog Caterpillar of the Grape-Vine. Royal Walnut Moth.*

At first Henrietta kept those creatures in plain glass tumblers, as she'd learned from a book that Daphne gave her: *Put your caterpillar upon a white paper, which you have first placed on an old book or other firm substance, and cover him with the glass. If you have several kinds at once, it is well to label the glasses. Write "Grape," or "Apple," or "Poplar" upon a slip of paper, and paste it upon the tumbler which covers that caterpillar you found upon the grape, apple, or other leaf. This will avoid confusion, as they one by one go into chrysalides. You can study each one separately, and you will know, as they come out of the chrysalides (which you have seen them make), just which is the moth of the grape, apple, or whatever your label indicates. You will thus know, also, at a moment's glance, how to feed them. They know what they want, which is more than can be said of some people.*

Henrietta, who in those days knew exactly what she wanted, quickly found this too simplistic, but she retained the obvious ideas, which she'd used in other areas, of labeling everything and keeping track of the caterpillars' food plants. Soon she corralled her friend Mason Perrotte into helping her build breeding cages, a foot square and eighteen inches tall, along two walls. Mason cut the glass and the wood, tacked the wire screening over the tops, sifted the dirt for the bases and cleaned out jars to hold the leafy branches. He made a display stand to entice the first members of Henrietta's Young Lepidopterists Club and later built smaller cases for her classroom. He left to Henrietta the preparation of the killing jars and the pinning of the specimens, but he kept good notes and his neat handwriting appeared on some of the labels. Until 1885, the year she shed Mason like an outgrown skin, he was an excellent helper.

THE YEARS IMMEDIATELY following Mason's departure were surprisingly calm, despite the unpleasant way in which they'd parted. Surprisingly happy. Hester startled Henrietta by marrying Ambrose Cummings, who owned the shoe and boot store in the village and was so quiet that Henrietta had hardly noticed him. At first things didn't change too much; they moved into a modest white house with red steps, a wide porch, a view of the Pleasant Valley through a frame of sturdy lilacs and trellised roses. Henrietta particularly liked that Hester's new place was barely a mile from their family home and an easy walk from the high school. She was helping out with a new kitchen cupboard one day, a few months after the wedding, when Hester announced that she was pregnant.

Ambrose hammered four nails in the wrong place while talking giddily about their hopes for several sons. Surreptitiously Henrietta inspected her sister's waist—but Hester had always been nicely plump, with rounded forearms and calves and a smooth, short neck, and she looked no different. The changes came after she lost that baby and then, several years later, another. (Exactly what Henrietta had dreaded; their own mother had lost several between herself and Hester.) Her hair thinned and her feet swelled, but the doctor couldn't figure out what was wrong and Henrietta feared she might be developing heart problems like those that now confined their mother to the house.

Perhaps, Henrietta suggested, Hester should avoid having children? But Hester said Henrietta understood nothing. Not about marriage, not about motherhood. "You're thirty-six," Hester pointed out then. "Without even a prospect."

And what was Henrietta supposed to say to that? Although she'd never told Hester about the painter Sebby Quint, her only regret about giving up Mason was the wreck of their long friendship and the gossip that had caused. Hester should have understood how limited her choices had otherwise been: only men crippled in one way or another, like Izzy Deverell, had returned from the war, and if Daphne had continued all this time with only the occasional gentleman friend, never settling into marriage, why shouldn't she? These days, when acquaintances nudged her toward plausible mates, she talked about her work and, if they pressed further, pointed out her obligations to her students and her family. Not just all her mother needed, but her deep involvement in her sister's life.

Which she could not, of course, say to her sister. Instead, as a way of counteracting Hester's growing despair and aimlessness, Henrietta begged for her help in the caterpillar room.

"I need another pair of hands," she said truthfully. "You'd be doing me a favor."

To her delight, Hester, who hadn't been interested in the caterpillars when she was a girl (she liked to sew, she liked to cook; she was a wizard gardener), agreed. Ambrose, who since Hester's second miscarriage had been devoting his spare time to raising and rebuilding a steamship sunk at the village dock, encouraged her in this.

"You're always finding caterpillars outside," he said. "Even when no one else notices them." Mostly he seemed relieved she might have something to do that didn't involve him.

One late July afternoon during Hester's first year helping out, Henrietta led her into the vegetable patch behind the house where their mother had once taught them to pick hornworms off the tomato leaves and toss them into the chicken coop. Now they gathered a dozen smaller hornworms, about an inch long: through their third molt, Henrietta explained, but not yet their fourth, so the young lepidopterists would still have plenty to see. She'd been telling them how an adult might lay eggs, a larva be induced to pupate; how a chrysalis, treated kindly, might in some months open to reveal a moth who might lay eggs. They might work out a creature's life history by starting anywhere.

Six little tin boxes for her six students; two caterpillars and a handful of fresh tomato leaves in each box: Hester helped with that. A few days later, the youngsters watched their caterpillars squirm and flex until the old skin burst behind the head and the face covering, pushed forward by the new, larger head, hung like a horse's feed bag. As the new caterpillars crawled from their old skins, the youngsters noted the date and the time each broke free. *Length 2 inches*, Eleanor wrote. *Pale-green head with white dots. Buff spiracles circled with black; long sharp horn in back; body bright green with yellow V-shaped markings. Very hungry!*

Mandy, shielding her neck as if the caterpillar might leap up and bite her, said uneasily that they ate as if they'd never stop. The leaves in the boxes melted away, transformed into green flesh. Soon the caterpillars were as long and thick as Henrietta's own substantial forefingers, and so strong that when Amy forgot to put the square of scrim Hester had given her over the tin box and under the lid, her caterpillars stood up on their hind prolegs and—were they *squeaking*?—pushed the lid off the box.

Thomasina quit the club after those heavy green heads poked out, but the others stalwartly added dirt to their boxes and watched the caterpillars burrow into it to emerge, two weeks later, as pulpy green pupae that hardened over a few hours into shapes they'd seen in their own gardens but not always recognized. Orestes marveled at the way the tube of the tongue case moved blindly through the air until the tip touched the wing covers and the whole structure solidified into a firm brown object, as shiny as a chestnut, with handsome curved segments and the tube containing the tongue arched back like the handle of a jug.

Later, after school started up, Henrietta showed those who continued in the club the five-spotted sphinx moths hatching out. The students sketched the black-encircled orange spots ornamenting each side of the torso and the soft gray back of the head. Mandy rendered the velvety eyes, but it was Hester, joining the youngsters, who captured the five-inch tongue unrolling and being shaken and then smoothed, like a lock of hair, before recurling into a little wheel.

Later, after they released the moths, they found one making a sound like a tiny drill as it drank from a stand of evening primroses.

"That's not a hummingbird?" Hester said, leaning in.

"Hummingbird moth," Henrietta said. "Watch." Four inches from the next flower the creature hovered—not dipping a long beak in for the nectar, but instead unfurling that marvelous tongue. Hester was so pleased by this that she volunteered to help once more in the spring of 1892, although she was pregnant again.

HENRIETTA KEPT HER worries to herself as Hester moved serenely through the months. Through June and July Hester collected and labeled caterpillars; in August and September she watched over the emerging moths and made sure they were mated before they laid their eggs. When Ambrose questioned her devotion, Hester swore that the atmosphere in the caterpillar room kept her healthy. At night, she told Henrietta, she sometimes wrapped her arms around her thickening torso and imagined her own body as a kind of sturdy pupa.

Was she joking? Henrietta, secretly appalled by that image, could not see even the trace of a smile on her sister's face. With one hand Hester cradled the swelling that was just beginning to show. No more lifting, bending, kneeling after that; Henrietta brought an armchair in for her sister, watched over her anxiously, and often went to her house in the evening to tend to the housework she didn't want Hester to do. When the being inside moved visibly beneath the taut cloth of Hester's dress, Henrietta tried not to imagine it bursting out.

Everything about the birth went easily, though. The snow sifted peaceably down to the frozen lake. The chickens roosted without complaint. While Henrietta helped the midwife, their mother sat near Hester's head and held her hand and Ambrose paced between the leafless apple trees. A few hours later Marion emerged, slick and wet and perfect. It was horrible to see her sister in pain, and yet to watch everything working as it should—a process she had seen before in cows and sheep and dogs, but never in a human—was also thrilling. Afterwards Henrietta brought her mother home and returned to find Hester and Marion already safely asleep.

By that spring, a young lepidopterist skirting the overgrown lilac might have seen through the windows of the caterpillar room a baby in a crate on the floor, looking among the other boxes filled with plants and dirt like a dahlia. A lovely child, everyone agreed. Marion fussed only when hungry or wet and seemed to enjoy the crate Henrietta had padded with towels and lined with calico. Hester, now convinced that nothing could be better for Marion than continued exposure to the habits of moths and butterflies, would, after nursing her, take up her perch on the stool and, leaning on the workbench, transcribe into a notebook the observations Henrietta dictated.

Surely, Henrietta thought, her niece gained some subtle benefit from watching her aunt and her mother work. By then Henrietta was training the brothers and sisters of her first pupils, and the caterpillar room was so familiar to the village that people dropped by with questions and treasures. A neighbor with a fritillary he'd caught in his cap. Young Sally Sazerat with a fat *Promethea* cocoon. Little boys brought gold-dotted emerald chrysalides attached to milkweed leaves; farm wives brought fat hornworms they'd plucked indignantly from ravaged tomatoes; Taggart Blake, a favorite student, brought a snowberry clearwing, which he'd mistaken for a gigantic bumblebee. Didier Durand, trailing his younger brother Jasper, brought a tiger swallowtail he thought was a monarch. Even after Marion began to crawl, and then to walk, Henrietta and Hester kept her in the caterpillar room when she was napping. When she woke, they brought her into the house, where their mother could watch her.

On an April Saturday in 1896, Henrietta got her first clue that

Marion might not be an only child. A few weeks earlier she'd brought her charges on an expedition she repeated every spring, searching for mourning cloak butterflies in the disappearing snow. Today she'd promised to show them the structure of the wings.

"We talked at our last meeting," she said, "about the mourning cloak's long life as an adult and its winter hibernation. Wiley and Sylvia were lucky enough to have their butterflies lay eggs, which are here on the willow twigs in our breeding cages. We'll be able to follow these as they develop into caterpillars through the summer and then pupate. The specimens that Jennie, Leander, and Carl gathered expired before they laid eggs—but they lived a long time for butterflies, almost ten months, and even dead they have something to teach us."

Behind her, Hester circled the worktable, offering each youngster two pieces of white notepaper before taking two for herself and settling down on the remaining stool. Henrietta followed with a tray of spread and pinned mourning cloaks. "They're so dark," she continued, laying one deep purplish-brown specimen at each place, "that it's even harder than usual to see the veins in the wings. We're going to remove the scales so we can see the venation clearly."

The air coming in through the partly opened windows was fresh and cool, smelling of earth and the granular snow still mounded in dark corners and against the walls. A cardinal was singing, some tufted titmice as well, as she showed Hester and the youngsters how to breathe on the top sheet of paper, lay it down over the butterfly wing on the bottom sheet, and then rub the top sheet gently with their fingernails. In that moment Henrietta was so happy she might have turned into a hummingbird moth herself.

"Lift the top papers gently," she said. "Now let those scales fall into the little glass dish next to you, breathe on the paper again, and repeat." Jennie smiled as the whole top wing became transparent, the veins standing out strongly. Henrietta pointed out the costal and subcostal veins, the multiple branches of the medial veins. Hester, who had done this exercise the previous spring, said from her end of the table, "I'm always amazed when this works." The youngsters drew diagrams as Henrietta passed out hand lenses and talked about the strength of the skeletons they'd uncovered.

After she had them look at some of the scales, she and Hester cleared everything away and then she brought out a little bottle of benzine, a paintbrush, and the last pinned specimen. "Here's something else we can do," she said. "When we have a rare specimen we don't want to destroy, we can still get a quick look at the veins without scraping the scales off."

She moistened a rag with the benzine and gently dabbed it over the wings. The color faded and then disappeared, leaving only the veins behind, their structure so clearly marked there might have been no scales at all. "Look quickly," she said, holding out her own hand lens. "It doesn't last."

She looked up as Hester made a noise and winced at the smell of the fumes. A few seconds later Hester backed away from the table with both hands pressed to her mouth, stepped outside, and bent over the window box.

CAROLINE WAS BORN that November: as difficult, from the moment she entered the world upside down, as Marion had been easy. For a night and a day Hester struggled to deliver her, so exhausted when Caroline's head finally followed her feet that she fainted. Hester had trouble feeding her; Caroline had trouble eating; she cried and cried and didn't gain weight and Henrietta feared she wouldn't survive. She seemed never to sleep. Hester developed mastitis and wept while she nursed. Caroline screamed and squirmed and tossed herself about so violently that Ambrose dropped her, twice, and after that refused to hold her. After six months she still weighed less than she should have but she was intensely alert, seeming to pay attention to everything. Often Henrietta could quiet her when no one else could, but even in Henrietta's arms she never snuggled the way Marion had. Always she was busy, always looking around.

Hester, confined to her bed for two months, wasn't herself even after she rose. The weight she'd gained carrying Caroline sat slackly, heavily, pooling around her hips and thighs without ever diminishing, and she now had trouble rising from a low chair or a stool. In the late afternoons, as soon as she could free herself from school, Henrietta began caring for Marion, either bringing her to the caterpillar room and entertaining her there, or taking her for walks in the woods, hoping that Hester might nap quietly with Caroline. Soon, though, Caroline stopped napping entirely.

What a temper she had! And what energy, pushing Marion away from Hester and, as she began to walk, darting off, breaking things, sometimes hurting her quieter sister. She grew like rhubarb, so quickly that at her grandmother's funeral in 1899, a stranger seeing the two little girls thought they were the same age. Marion, holding one of Henrietta's hands, walked quietly, but Caroline pulled so violently at Henrietta's other hand that she couldn't steady Hester, who during their mother's last days had miscarried yet again.

Writing to her friend Daphne, who by then had met Hester several times, Henrietta described how Hester had tottered through the funeral. *How many times does she have to go through this?* she wrote. *Why don't she and Ambrose just stop? Ambrose is useless and every year she gets less like herself, less like the girl I grew up with—although I guess this new person is also her "self." I don't feel like you and I have changed that violently, though. Is it just having children?* Then she took another sheet of paper and, as if that gave her a clean new life, wrote to the naturalist Anna Comstock without saying a single word about her family.

I'd be delighted to write some "Nature Study" leaflets for your series, she wrote. *After more than two decades of teaching high school and also running an extracurricular Young Lepidopterists Club in our village, I know how to interest children in the outside world and could devise standardized lessons any teacher might find useful as she begins her own program of Nature Study. I imagine one leaflet about the general study of moths and butterflies. Another, perhaps—drawing on the excellent work of Samuel Scudder, which I know has often inspired you—about the study of monarch migration. Others might follow, if these suited.*

Or they'd follow, if she found the time—what had happened to her time? She taught her classes and prepared new classes; ran her labs and devised laboratory exercises; worked on projects with certain former students, especially Bernard. She directed this club, for which, since she'd started encouraging young pupils, she now had to design new projects. She tended her house and her garden and the caterpillar room while also, especially after Hester got pregnant again, helping care for Marion and Caroline. But this was important, and as soon as she heard back from Anna Comstock, she stole time to begin drafting a Nature Study leaflet she titled "Caterpillars and Their Moths."

Not just an explanation of the life cycles of some common moths, but a way to shift the students' focus from the glamorous winged forms, which often lived only a few days, to the resourceful crawling state in which they really spent most of their lives. The little worms hatching out of their eggs; the busily feeding middle instars with their fascinating molts; the fat creatures, decorated with hairs and tubercles and horns; and finally the astonishing transformations as they pupated—any schoolchild would be drawn to these. She wrote some introductory pages about necessary equipment and the rudiments of caterpillar anatomy and physiology, and in a separate notebook listed possible candidates for full life histories. Hornworms, which turn into hawkmoths. Hog caterpillars, which turn into fat-bodied Nessus sphinx moths. Perhaps the yellow-headed caterpillars with knobs first yellow and later red, emerging from leaf-wrapped cocoons as gigantic *Promethea* silk moths? All easily found, appealing to any young naturalist. But before she could begin work on those, Elaine was born: a month early, tiny but strong, with a cry so piercing she seemed to sense this would be the only way to get what she needed.

Daphne came to visit that August, when Elaine was still nursing. After an uncomfortable supper at Hester's house, Henrietta was reminded of how her sister's life might look through other eyes: loud, messy, difficult, exhausting. Caroline chasing Marion up the stairs—was Caroline holding a fork? Marion hiding Caroline's favorite toy, while Caroline shrieked. Elaine crying to be fed and then, after spitting up, crying again as her two older sisters quarreled in dangerously quiet tones. Caroline knocking over a coffee cup, stepping into the dark puddle, and then claiming it was an accident.

To Daphne, later, Henrietta apologized for the chaotic evening but then, thinking how Daphne's presence had diverted her own attention, which might have caused some of the girls' misbehavior, said, "I love being around my nieces, though. Even when they're difficult."

She couldn't say to Daphne (she couldn't admit it to herself) that what she felt for her nieces was largely the overflow of her fierce love for Hester. The girls were splinters of Hester, offshoots of Hester. It would take a few years before she'd learn to love them (some more than others) for themselves.

"It's not my business," Daphne said coolly: always solitary, never involved with her family more than superficially. Henrietta hadn't met a single one of Daphne's relatives and did not, she realized, even know most of their names.

SPRING AGAIN—AND STILL, as Daphne pointed out, the cater-pillar booklet wasn't done. Still, Hester wasn't back to her old self, which meant that now Henrietta spent most late afternoons and early evenings at her sister's house, helping make supper and feed her nieces, doing housework that Hester could no longer manage and that Ambrose, caught up now in some attempts by his friends to motorize a bicycle, ignored. Often she brought Marion, who at nine was the same age as some of the younger pupils, to meet-ings of her young lepidopterists. She was not, Henrietta had to acknowledge, particularly interested in moths or other small crea-tures—bugs were crawly, frogs were slimy, snakes slithered, mice jumped. But as she liked being around her school friends and also liked flowering plants, Henrietta put her in charge of determining the names and growing habits of the plants the other children's caterpillars ate.

Sometimes Hester was so exhausted that she begged Henrietta to take Caroline with her too, so that she could nap with Elaine. At five, Caroline was too young to sit still for long or to manage the tools the older children used—but she was genuinely fascinated by the caterpillars and moths. She made the room untidy, she rup-tured Henrietta's careful plans (where had the calm days with Hester gone?), but still her interest was thrilling. *Why?* she asked, through-out the afternoons. Why did the caterpillars shed their skins? Why did some eat their shed skins, and why were the heads first too big and then too small, and why did some have horns? She tore open a chrysalis when Henrietta wasn't looking, prying inside with a sharp stick: Why couldn't she find the moth growing in there, what was all that jelly? Henrietta had to guard against neglecting the others while devoting too much attention to Caroline's questions and try-ing to explain to her what an experiment was, and how it was use-ful. Exhausting, that curiosity. Annoying—but also delightful. Less delightful was the pained look on Marion's face when she saw her sister absorbing so much of Henrietta's time.

HENCE THE ROSY maple moths of that afternoon's session: an offering. Pleasing in their color and texture if not their shape, a way of showing that Henrietta cared what Marion liked. She hadn't counted on having Elaine with her that afternoon, though. Nor on Caroline being so curious about the wiggling pupae. As she tucked Elaine more securely into the crate on the floor, Henrietta looked into Caroline's eyes and emphasized her responsibility again.

"Just *you*," she repeated.

Caroline nodded, even as Henrietta resolved to watch the pair closely. The box was the same as when Marion had used it, but everything else was different. No Hester, working with her companionably. No beloved mother in the house across the garden, ready to take over if a baby cried. And all her youngsters this year were young.

Eager, though, and intelligent: Emily, Franklin, Clover, and James had helped Henrietta collect a heap of green-striped mapleworms last fall, decanting them carefully into shallow trays of earth that they dotted with maple leaves. They'd watched the redheaded worms burrow into the dirt and transform into slim dark pupae, but then, after Henrietta tucked the trays in the root cellar, forgotten about them over the winter. Now they were thrilled to see them wake in the warm room. Clover touched the pointed fork on one and said, "Look! It moved!" And then Franklin said, "That one's cracking open!"

Marion pushed her way nearer as the crack widened and the wet moth began to work its way out. The head, the bedraggled antennae; the front legs and then the bulge of the damply furred back; soon the entire moth emerged, tottered over to climb the twig Henrietta had stuck in the dirt and, clinging head upward, began to unfold its wings. So pink, so yellow! Marion smiled as if presented with the little peony the moth resembled and watched without speaking as the fluid pumping through the veins began to expand the crumpled membranes.

Clover and Emily timed the stages and took notes; Franklin sketched several views of the process; James remembered to check the other pupae and was rewarded by spotting a second one beginning to eclose. Marion continued to watch the first moth, which grew lovelier by the minute, with an interest that pleased Henrietta until Clover raised her head, looked past Henrietta's shoulder, and said, in a startled voice, "Should she be doing that?"

Henrietta turned to follow Clover's gaze and then with two quick strides reached Elaine's empty box. Bent stomach-down over Caroline's knees, Elaine lay quite still, neither crying nor squirming: such a good baby, always. Caroline—where had she gotten *scissors?*—was using one hand to press down the back of Elaine's head and the other to control the sharp blades. The top blade, pointed toward Elaine's feet, was visible above the cotton blanket enclosing her; the other was under—oh, let it only be under the blanket and the dress!

Henrietta slid the scissors out, dropped them to the floor, and then seized Elaine and parted the cut fabric. A scratch ran from the base of the baby's neck a few inches along her spine, not all the way through the skin except in one place, about an inch down, which oozed a bright drop of blood. When Henrietta pressed the tip of her finger there, Elaine finally wailed. Only then did Henrietta let herself look at Caroline.

"What—?" Henrietta said. She was breathing so quickly she thought she might faint. "What—?"

Caroline stood up. "I was *turning* her," she explained patiently. Bending down, she reached for the scissors—but there was Marion, knocking Caroline's arm away. She seized the scissors herself, she closed the blades. She held the instrument by the points, looking as if she wished it were a stiletto.

"Why do you *always*—?" she said to her sister.

As calmly as she could, Henrietta told her to sit with the others. Then she said, to Caroline, "What do you mean, 'turning her'?"

"Into a person," Caroline explained. "Someone who can talk and play with me. Like the caterpillar turns into the brown thing. Like the brown thing turns into the moth. An experiment, like you said, so—the skin always opens there, right at the back of the neck. I thought if I opened Elaine's wrapping, she might come out sooner."

The noise Henrietta heard from the table was, she realized, Marion jabbing the points of the scissors into the wood. *Hester,* Henrietta thought. Where was Hester, where was Hester?

THE ACCIDENT

DAPHNE SAW THE POSTER FOR THE AIR SHOW EARLY IN August 1922, a week before the county fair in her corner of Massachusetts and a few months after her seventy-fifth birthday. Her health had improved so enormously that to celebrate she'd bought a new Ford runabout and learned to drive it: what pleasure, now, to have the strength and energy to plan a route and manage the wheel! Sixteen miles in good weather was nothing to her, and the advertised stunts were alluring. Also she wanted to see the military surplus aeroplanes, which had been designed in the village where Henrietta lived—and most especially one of the aviators, who was Henrietta's niece.

Caroline Cummings: a vibrant, troublesome, courageous little girl, or so Daphne remembered her. A girl who'd left home young, traveled widely, and since the war (did she have this right? She hadn't seen Caroline in eight or nine years, but she paid attention to Henrietta's stories) had made her living as a barnstormer. Once Daphne had believed that Henrietta would show that kind of daring. But these days she could not even lure Henrietta into sharing a vacation.

The road winding down from the hill towns into the broad Connecticut Valley was smooth and quiet, the air so still that Daphne heard animals calling and crying in the agricultural halls before she reached the fairground. From an aproned woman she bought a sandwich and then inspected the sheep (especially nice were the Romney ewes), the rabbits, the dairy cows and the draft oxen. Later she walked through the tables of jams and the pickles and pies; still later she admired the roses and the dahlias. Half an hour before the air show's start, she found a seat in the stands beside the improvised runway and settled herself with her broad-brimmed hat and a cushion. The men who made up most of the crowd made room for her as politely as if she were old. Three planes bumped along the field, took off together, flew side by side and then parted and circled high above. A man climbed up on the left-hand plane's upper wing while a second plane drew terrifyingly close. Before Daphne could be sure what was happening, the wing walker swung himself by a rope from his plane to the other, which peeled away as the third plane, as if applauding, made a long, slow backflip, nose over tail over nose.

An inside loop, Daphne learned, when the aircraft pulled away and she had a second to consult her program. The pilots were nearly invisible, their helmeted and goggled heads identical dots at this distance—but the person who'd done the loop was apparently Caroline. The planes came back over the field, two flying side by side but now with a wing walker on each machine. The walkers faced each other and danced in unison on their respective wings, then dropped at the same time to dangle by their knees from bars below the struts. Daphne turned from them to concentrate instead on the shapely patterns Caroline carved through the sky behind them. A barrel roll, an outside loop; then a complicated shape, part loop and part roll, that the program identified as an Immelmann turn—how was it the engine didn't stall, the plane didn't fall from the sky? She had no idea when she stood up, or why she was craning her neck as if to get closer to the maneuvers. By the time the show concluded, she was exhausted.

Daphne waited until the crowd had cleared before walking over

to the hangar and introducing herself to Caroline. Beneath her hel-
met Caroline's hair was cropped, her face marked by an unusual set
of scars. Her sharp eyes, deeply set and shadowed, scanned Daphne's
features repeatedly, but she was sufficiently well mannered to act as
if she remembered her aunt's favorite friend.

Perhaps she did, or perhaps her combined exhaustion and
exhilaration was what made her so nervously talkative, so confid-
ing. Daphne, expecting no more than a routine answer—surely
Caroline had been asked this a hundred times?—asked what she
most wanted to know, which was how Caroline had started flying.
The long, peculiarly intimate story that emerged, carrying the two
women back across the field, into Daphne's runabout, to the picnic
table at the ice cream store, where they ate peach ice cream and
brushed away the thickening mosquitoes, vibrated with the pain of a
fox crying for a lost pup. Or of Henrietta unspooling her dreams and
disappointments during their first passionate conversations, when
they were capturing horseshoe crabs on an island in Buzzards Bay.

Although Daphne tried to remember every phrase as Caroline
had conveyed it, it's possible that her own feelings and her understanding of her friend's family amplified some elements, intensi-
fied some emotions. Maybe she smoothed out Caroline's syntax or
altered her vocabulary. Still, she believed that Caroline said this—

I DON'T KNOW what went on in town those first few days. I didn't
see the reporters chasing the story or the neighbors my parents
turned away. I was seventeen; I had a snail named Samuel who lived
in a jar with a bit of dirt from the forest; I wore hand-me-downs and
had odd habits and not many friends. Until that summer, my family
had kept me busy, in both good ways and bad. For the week after the
accident, almost all I did was sleep.

In my dreams, I was running up the path at the side of the Glen, picking grapes on Bully Hill, driving a buggy, swimming under the dock. I was at school, under Aunt Henrietta's watchful eye; I was dressing one of the twins; I was flipping pancakes or lifting grapes from crates and repacking them into baskets. I was dancing. I was skating near the hotel where the parties were held; I was ducking one little sister into the water or walking the shore with another. But when I woke, I was always in bed, both legs and one arm stiffly casted, my head bandaged, the left side of my mouth and face sliced past the cheekbone to the place where a chunk of my scalp was gone.

This was during the grape harvest of 1913, when everyone in the village was busy and accidents at the wineries—a hand caught in a crusher, a full crate dropped onto a foot—were so common that the doctor was already working night and day. My right thigh and left shin were broken; I'd fallen twelve feet when the aeroplane scraped me from the canvas hangar. Where the wing hit—I'd raised my right arm—both bones broke between wrist and elbow, and also some ribs, but because my arm had partly shielded my head, the propeller slashed my face at an angle instead of hitting straight on. I couldn't see because of the bandage over my nicked eyelids, but the doctor said my eyes weren't damaged and I wasn't blind. Bluntly, and too soon, he also said that Link had crashed his machine after hitting us, but he was alive and not badly hurt. Raney's friends, the two Navy lieutenants who'd pulled us up onto the ridgepole, had walked away with cuts and bruises. Raney was dead.

I slept, woke, slept and woke again: and still, Raney was dead. I dreamed about the red silk wings of the first flying machine I ever saw, rising briefly above the frozen lake. I dreamed I was flying a glider, and then that Constantine Boyd, a little boy I knew, had built me my own aeroplane. I dreamed that my father brought me black kid boots, as elegant as Raney's, magically fitting my swollen feet—and I dreamed about Raney, a large fair girl with straight hair hardly darker than champagne. The first time I'd seen her, she was sitting on the dock of her family's summer place, talking with her friends as I watched my sisters at the town beach. I'd pretended not to notice her.

Soon the door would open, bang shut, open and open again— Elaine, who was supposed to wait for the twins but seldom did, followed by Agnes and Alice. After crashing around, dropping their books, rushing into the kitchen for something to eat, my younger sisters would tiptoe into what had been the dining room but was now given over to me and the borrowed bed. My feet toward the kitchen, my head against the wall. My broken legs lined up with the windows that opened to the porch, and beside me, on the floor, the heavy glass jar that had once held specimens for my aunt's biology class. *Caroline*, Elaine would whisper, *are you awake? I'm giving Samuel a leaf.* Her job, now, to take care of him. Then Alice would sit on the piano bench and tell me what she'd done at school, and our older sister, Marion, would crash pots in the sink as she waited for our aunt's arrival to release her. She had work at one of the vineyards and couldn't stand tending me.

Before she graduated, Marion had been an excellent student, and I'd followed in her footsteps, always doing more than required and never cutting class. But on the day of the accident, Raney had looked at me scornfully when I'd first refused her invitation and said, "I never thought you'd be a *coward*," so upsetting me that I'd walked the twins to the main door, gone to my classroom, claimed a stomachache and walked back out. Partly I still wanted to please her. Partly I couldn't stand for her to do one more daring thing without me. She loaned me a dress so I wouldn't have to wear my everyday waist and skirt, and we ran to the boardinghouse where the two Navy aviators she knew were waiting to take us for a ride in a motorboat. Palmer, who was taller and had a wonderful nose, took the picnic basket from Raney. Elly lifted a canvas tote and said, "That blue suits your eyes." We were almost at the dock when Palmer stopped and turned his head toward a buzzing sound. "I'll be damned!" he said. "He's taking the new one up."

"Who?" I said. "What?"

He pointed to an aeroplane rising from the field.

"That's Link," Palmer said, referring to a famous flyer who dropped by now and then but hadn't been around for some months. "Want to go see?"

"Why not?" Raney said. We'd been watching the flights all summer but neither of us had seen Link perform and Elly said his machine was brand new.

As we crossed the flats, Link landed and then took off again. A crowd of curious people swarmed across the grass, surrounding the machine when it touched back down. Palmer, or maybe Elly, said it was always worth watching Link fly. Elly, or maybe Palmer, pointed to the canvas tent sheltering the hydro-aeroplanes.

"Sometimes we watch each other from the ridgepole," he said. "Great view—think you can follow me up?"

Maybe I nodded. Maybe I showed him my sturdy wrists. Raney, when he turned to her, said, "You bet."

Later, lots of people would tell me how the accident had looked to them. None of them would be Link, who came to the hospital along with Elly and Palmer to see my broken body but then fainted next to the bed where I lay unconscious. They dropped him off at the train station the following week, when they had to return to their base at Annapolis, and I never did get to talk to him. Eighteen months later he was dead, first the right and then the left wing of another machine snapping off as he came around the top of a loop and crashed into San Francisco Bay—but on the afternoon we shared, the air was still, the lake serene, and the field initially empty, but for him. Quiet and calm, Kingsley Flats dry, the hangar tent free of Navy officers. *On this day, October 7, 1913, I wanted, before flying at the Aeronautical Society's celebration of a decade of mechanical flight, to try out this new machine privately and quietly*, he'd tell the news papermen while my eyes were still bandaged. *I was not attempting to loop the loop nor to do any other extraordinary feat at the time.*

Someone brought me that clipping, but I wouldn't have blamed him even if I hadn't seen it. He'd meant to have a simple flying day: start the engine with the help of a workman, roll over the ground, rise into the air. Everything the same as always. Below him our village square—he'd dip a wing over his boardinghouse—and also the Depot, the steamboat docks, the sailboats, the vineyards climbing the hills. Then the aeroplane factory and the half-built machines, the train headed down the valley to Bath—and the place where he'd tested the new dirigible engine, and the places where he'd crashed his first machine and then the others, and the tavern where—

Suddenly the field was full of people. He'd hoped to keep this private, but he hadn't flown in months and word that he'd gone up spread quickly. More people were leaving their houses and shops and crossing the streets, three motorboats were trailing him in the water below, everyone was charging toward the cluster of hangars on the shoreline, crowding the field so densely he could hardly find a place to land. What did they think he was going to do? Thin white clouds hung high above, while smaller tufts started moving below: wind. The machine felt heavy, but still better than last year's tractor model. Was it his fault so many men had died trying to imitate the tricks he'd invented? His vertical glide, which the newspapers liked to call the Dip of Death. His Dutch Roll, his Figure Eight: easy for him, disastrous for inexperienced men flying machines they hardly knew. The wives wrote terrible letters to him; the newspapers pounded at him. In March he'd announced his retirement. Then (this was in the papers, too) he'd learned that a French aviator had flown a loop, which so many thought impossible. How infuriating! That was *his* trick, surely; who was better equipped? Within weeks he'd ordered a new machine from the factory. This one should fly upside down no matter what—but it did feel heavy, dipping in the rising wind, and he turned over the water again and headed back toward land.

Annoying to have so many people in the field. And to see, on the ridgepole of the largest tent, still more observers: Elly and Palmer, who often watched from there, with two figures he didn't recognize. Palmer flourished his cap and reached for a girl in a light dress. Then all four figures waved. He was fifty feet above the water when he turned to line his nose up with the clear patch of field, and then he was close enough to the tent to see a girl point a camera at him. And then—

An air pocket, a downward gust, too much headway lost when he turned? He dropped hard, struggling to clear the tent, his own mouth opening as Palmer jumped from the ridgepole and slid down the canvas, reaching to pull Raney after him. A thump—something hitting the ridgepole—two thuds, a clatter, the pull of gravity, the crunch of bamboo collapsing around him and then he was upside down, hanging from his shoulder straps, caged in broken struts and shredded cloth, the engine still sputtering behind him. Pants and shoes and skirt hems and boots, a dog nosing past a tangle of wire. What had been his front wheel spun slowly above; his top wing lay crushed below his head. His feet were pointed at the sky. Someone was crying, someone screamed twice and was silent, someone cursed steadily and savagely as someone else begged for him to stop. He'd swept the people from the tent, he heard. Both men were hurt, but they could walk. His own hands could open and shut but he didn't know what to do with them. His wings had hit the girls, he heard:

one was dead and the other—me—was badly hurt. He couldn't see them or the hangar or the blood sprayed around, the automobile dented by the falling girl, the doctor who pronounced the other girl dead. Only the legs surrounding him, and a bit of sky, and his front wheel. Someone reached through the wreckage with a knife, to cut his shoulder straps and pull him free, but even before the knife touched leather he could feel the hands of the souvenir hunters tearing off scraps of the cloth. My aunt still has some of the postcards Mr. Benner made from this scene.

BUT HERE I'M getting ahead of myself, or behind myself: I was in bed. My father was absent, as always. Upstairs our mother's bed creaked; she'd been an invalid since the twins were born, nearly half my life. For a long time Aunt Henrietta had come to help in the late afternoons, after she finished teaching school; that was when she'd first brought us Samuel, or the first Samuel, so deftly swapping the quick for the dead over time that we could believe—Agnes and Alice still believed—he was a single, remarkably long-lived snail. Eventually Marion and I had taken over most of the housework. Now, while I waited for time to pass and the bone fragments to knit themselves to each other, the cooking and cleaning had fallen back on Marion, who was furious with me. Femur, the bone in my thigh. Tibia, the bone in my shin; ulna and radius in my arm. In my bed in the dining room I heard the doors open and close and felt a strip of shadow over my throat: my aunt, who always seemed to smell like a fern, stretching a cool hand down to where the stitches itched and pulled.

She'd brought me not schoolwork, which I could make up later, but Amundsen's account of his expedition to the South Pole, which she'd extravagantly purchased so she could read to me for a couple of hours every afternoon. The volumes were blue, she said. Gilded edges, lots of maps and photographs; before long I'd see them for myself. *Here I am*, the first chapter began, *sitting in the shade of palms, surrounded by the most wonderful vegetation, enjoying the most magnificent fruits, and writing—the history of the South Pole!* Which meant that Amundsen knew, as I now had to learn, the secret of sending his imagination to one place while his body was someplace else. *One circumstance has followed on the heels of another, and everything has turned out so entirely different from what I had imagined* . . .

On the tenth day after the accident, the doctor came, re-dressed the wound on my head, tended the stitches on my face, and then unwrapped my eyes. First warmth, then light: then—everything. The sky, the clouds, the glinting lake, Samuel tucked beside a fern, my hands and legs—I turned away from the casts—the sky! Almost at once my eyes began to itch, burn, drip tears, but the doctor said this was normal, I'd be sensitive to light for a while.

Marion was out and Aunt Henrietta was still at school, but my mother returned after the doctor left. Her face, which I was so glad to see, was more deeply lined than I remembered, and she reached over and smoothed the bandage on my head when I asked her for a mirror.

"You could wait," she said. "There's no hurry."

"Now," I said.

She went and fetched her hand mirror, along with a glass of water. "It's temporary," she said. "It'll get better."

Nothing was left of my long dark hair except a rough fringe below the bandages, but I'd already felt that with my hand; my hair would grow back. The black circles around my eyes would disappear, the nicks in my eyebrows would fill in, the scabs on my eyelids would vanish. The long row of black stitches crossing the raised red flesh on my chin, through the corner of my mouth, over my cheek and cheekbone and into my temple—that would leave a scar. And where the stitches disappeared, under the edge of the bandage, I had no hair at all.

"Don't cry," my mother said.

I wasn't crying; the tears were from the glare. I turned my head, inspecting the damage. Some would improve, some wouldn't: I was alive. I had been pleasant-looking, unremarkable. Now I was different. I put the mirror down and feasted my eyes on the view from the window.

Then on my aunt's face, when she arrived; on my sisters and my father. The newspaper turned in my father's hands. The steam rose from a chicken. Alice, beautiful Alice, braided Agnes's hair, and at dusk the swallows gathered and darted, as if at a signal, into their nests. After everyone went to bed I stayed up for a long time, watching the moon on the trees and the shadows below. The next day I read a few pages of Aunt Henrietta's gift and saw the wonderful maps with my own eyes. Amundsen had delayed until they reached Madeira telling his crew that they were not heading north, as he'd announced, but toward the opposite pole. *It must be admitted that it was a big risk*, he wrote, *but there were so many risks that had to be taken at the time.* From that I might have learned something about the timing of announcements.

WHEN I WAS a little girl, I saw dirigibles rise from unexpected places often enough to think that normal. Trudging up a snowy hill with my sled, I passed gleeful strangers running down with gliders and hoping to take off, and I saw the first crashes of the first aeroplanes. With my sisters and Aunt Henrietta and Constantine Boyd, I watched the *June Bug* rise from the bumpy field to claim the great prize. Reporters hung around then as well, eager to glimpse the newest models, always hoping to be the first to the site of an accident. Photographers made postcards out of the crashes, which drew more young flyers from France and Spain, Russia and Cuba, New Jersey and California. The boardinghouses were packed; the market stocked strange groceries; my father made boots for them. Everyone sought out the men at the flying school.

On good days we fly, on rainy days we learn why—the flying school motto, which all of us knew. The flyers gathered at the edge of the lake before the sun was up; took off while the air was calm; landed before most of us were fully awake. By the time I was in high school, a hundred men were working in the aeroplane factory and every session at the flying school was packed. Because the aeroplane's designer had managed to interest the Navy Department in the idea of a machine that could take off and land on water, contractors and naval officers (Palmer was one of those, Elly another) came and went as well. The instructors worked from dawn until the sun was fully set, darning together the shores of the lake.

When the men weren't flying or tinkering with their machines, playing cards or drinking together, they went to the parties thrown for them by our wealthy families and summer people. Raney's father, proud of what they called their cottage—two kitchens, a double-sized reception room that opened to a long porch perched over a private beach, a swim float and a wooden dock with padded pilings and room to tie up several boats—hosted several each summer. Middle-aged men and women from Rochester and Corning and Syracuse circled among young flyers from all over the world, instructors from the flying school, and a few of the wealthier neighbors. If the wind was right, you could hear them laughing from the beach where I brought my sisters.

I'd imagined the inside of that cottage as looking like a magazine advertisement, all gleaming wood and thick, soft carpets, but when Raney first invited me over, I saw how wrong I'd been. Everything was new but designed to look old, the furnishings meant to suggest the rustic without being actually uncomfortable. "You think that's silly," she said, watching me trace the unpeeled birch branches forming a chair frame.

"Hard to dust," I observed. When she laughed and pointed out the twisted vine trunks supporting a tabletop and the chandelier's frosted-glass globes, shaped like clusters of grapes, I thought we might be real friends. All summer I held on to that, even though sometimes, as I entered parties and dances at her side only to lose her as she was swarmed, I'd wonder what she wanted me for. Men talked about flying while their eyes moved from Raney's arms to Raney's chest to Raney's eyes and hair.

I remember slipping down the porch stairs at one party, sitting on a bench bolted to the dock as I listened to the voices hum: *Raaaaaay-nee. Raaaaaaaaaa-nee.* All those men. Farther out on the dock was the only one not paying attention to her, a Dutch flyer I'd met once or twice before (this was Adrien Hendricks, but at the time I didn't know his name). Headed his way, after half an hour of trying in vain to get Raney's attention, was Jasper Durand. Tall, dark-haired, sharp-nosed like all the Durands, he was also uniquely pigeon-toed, which gave his walk an interesting sway. He looked so unhappy that as he passed I almost said something to him. I didn't, though—his family owned one of the largest wineries in town, and his circle didn't intersect much with mine—and he continued down the dock to Adrien. I went home before they left, not expecting to see them again except in passing.

Jasper surprised me, though, both by his persistence with Raney and by showing up after the accident. He arrived with an envelope, which he first held out but then, seeing my casts, opened himself. I read the letter twice before letting it fall to the quilt.

"You know what it says?"

"I do," he replied. "I hope it's all right." His grandmother's large, forceful script expressed the family's sympathy and then announced that they, along with several other winery families, had settled my hospital bills in Bath.

"That's—wonderful," I said. My aunt had thought Link might offer to pay, but he hadn't, and my father had been frantic. "So generous." Jasper nodded politely and rose from the chair. "Would you thank your grandmother, from all of us?"

"Of course," he said. He leaned over toward the big glass jar and tapped the rim. "Terrarium?"

"Aunt Henrietta," I said, knowing she'd taught him in high school.

He nodded, said, "I loved her class," and left, looking as if he wanted to say something else.

That night my mother read the note and said vaguely how kind this was—the same words with which, for years, she'd accepted our neighbors' help when she was confined to bed, and everything my aunt did every day. My father flushed, flicked the paper off the table, and then retrieved it, muttering, "I suppose we'll have to take it." My aunt wrote the thank-you letter. I didn't expect that I'd see Jasper again, but a few days later he showed up with a potted fern and offered to read to me.

"It's hard for you to turn pages," he said. He seemed pleased to have noticed this.

"True enough," I said.

My aunt had reached the part in the blue volumes where Amundsen recounted his arrival at the Pole, and Jasper picked up where she'd left off and read for ten minutes. Then he put down the book and said, "He finally got what he wanted, after all." Through the window I saw both the golden willow twigs and also a white landscape scored with ski tracks, the dogs' curled tails moving steadily toward the horizon. I longed for him to keep reading. "Meanwhile I do what my family wants. Raney . . ."

And there it was. I knew that he'd been seeing her, but not that he'd been aware of her for so long. His father and hers, he said, had worked together on several community events, and because her mother was dead, and her father was busy, she did exactly as she pleased. When she was fourteen, fifteen, sixteen (I couldn't remember seeing her then, I'd first noticed her the summer she was seventeen), she used to walk down the road to the Durands' winery and visit him in the laboratory where, when he was in college, he helped out during the summers.

"Mostly to tease me, I think," Jasper said. "And because she was bored. She liked to see if she could rattle me when I was doing something complicated."

I murmured politely each time he paused. Finally he stopped and said, "Your face looks better," as if, after being interested in me only because I knew Raney, he'd suddenly decided that we were friends.

I touched my slashed cheek. Now that the stitches were out I felt less conspicuous, but the flesh was still inflamed and one of the smaller cuts, which went clear through my eyebrow, was infected. My aunt had been treating me with salve she'd made from some plant in the woods, but that lid was still swollen, closing the outer corner of my eye, and my hair—I was trying not to think about the bald patch.

"Do you think?" I said.

"You were lucky," he said. "Really." He caught himself, stood up and crossed to the window. "The last time I saw Raney alone . . ."

He stopped and pressed his forehead to the glass. A few crows crossed the heavy sky; the leaves were down and soon there'd be frost. I'd been in bed when the leaves were on the trees and would still be there when the snow fell, piled up, packed down, turned to ice and then was covered by more; I'd be there when the snow began to melt. Five months, the doctor had said, before I'd be walking easily.

"Sorry," Jasper said faintly.

"Why don't you read?" I suggested. I knew some of what had happened the last time he saw Raney alone and I didn't want to hear more. "We could both use the distraction."

"I'd rather talk," he said. "I can't talk with anyone else. You know how people in town feel about her family."

Summer people; pushy strangers dripping city money: I knew. I also knew how much people like us depended on that money. I had classmates who cleaned their houses, pruned their shrubs, tended their boats and docks. My father stocked special hobnailed boots to tempt the bankers who wanted to hike. Raney's first words to me, early that summer, had been a request to grab the line she tossed from her sailboat to the dock where I was standing. I was carrying a box of twine I'd picked up for my father, and she might have thought I worked at the boatyard. When she asked me later if I'd like to sail with her, I thought at first she was offering me work.

Instead we sailed across the lake to dances, we swam together, we picked berries and made ice cream and met college boys and out-of-town flyers at parties and band concerts. I slipped away from my sisters to join her every chance I got. She didn't follow our rules; she acted like they didn't exist—and from out of all the others, she'd chosen me. Me, to confide in, and misbehave with, and join her in flirting with the intriguing visitors who normally would have ignored me.

I'd turned my back on everyone else and then, when she returned to Rochester at the end of August, been stupidly surprised to find that my classmates, who since first grade had been inhaling the same dust in the same rooms where the same clocks moved too slowly, thought of me as a defector. A few of them, not kindly, let me know

I'd only been that summer's friend, picked as others had been in other years, to be dropped eight weeks later.

I wrote her four times after she left. She didn't answer until she came back with her father in early October. The note she sent then gave me hope. She was bored, she wrote. So bored! What should we do? I was offended, I was delighted, I wanted to snub her, I wanted to see her. I couldn't meet her on the Saturday she came back—I was washing bottles at Whitcomb's that day, and I was anxious to pile up my earnings while the weather held—but I said I'd meet her at the dance that night.

After I brought in my last boxes, I walked home by the path at the base of the hill, behind the yards attached to the handsome houses. Jasper, his parents, and the rest of his sprawling family lived in one, with a huge back garden where I sometimes saw his grandmother or his ancient aunts. A lawn stretched toward the path from the rose bed, sinking damply as it neared the gazebo. From there someone whispered, "Go ahead. Come on."

Not his elderly relatives but a girl's voice, a teasing laugh.

Then, "Don't," I heard. "Don't you . . ."

A man, not laughing. Against the gazebo's back wall, Jasper was entangled with another pair of arms and hands, a swirl of skirts. A bit of white gleamed in the dusky light: a breast, perhaps; the girl's shirtwaist was all the way open. The heads bent together, stayed together. I backed toward the hill until I was off the path entirely, my boots in the ferns, but I couldn't make myself move on. The girl was Raney.

Jasper said, "Is that fun for you? To tease me like that?"

"Do what you want," she said. "You know I'd let you."

Jasper pulled away a couple of inches, his hands still reaching toward Raney but neither touching her nor resting at his own sides. Just—stuck there, stupidly. "I'd marry you, if you wanted," he said.

The noise I made then was covered by Raney's scornful laugh. "As if I'd ever live in this ridiculous place—I want to leave Rochester for someplace *larger*, not smaller. I come because it's a change from home. And because my father's too busy when he's here to notice what I do. Anyway"—she flicked at one of Jasper's frozen hands—"can't you just have some fun? Enjoy what we have?"

"What makes you think I'm staying here?" he said. "Maybe *I* want to go someplace larger."

"You won't," she said.

"I will," he insisted.

"We'll see. But for now, let's just . . ." She moved toward him again, pressing her whole length against him so urgently that I flushed.

"Stop it," Jasper said.

"Why?" Without meaning to, I'd inched closer and I had to catch myself. "It's not like you're the only one."

"I know." His voice caught. "Although I was hoping you might take me a little more seriously, and that maybe I *could* be the only one. I'm not interested in being part of the crowd you flirt with."

I bolted then, feeling too much like Jasper; I wanted to be the only one so badly I was sick. When Raney had first plucked me from the dock, I'd thought that meant I was special. Even if only specially good at helping her get what she wanted.

That night I didn't go to the dance; the next day we met at the baseball game but I was too uneasy with my glimpse of her and Jasper. A few days later I skipped school as she asked and felt like nothing had changed between us. And then she was gone. She was gone, I was in bed, and Jasper was walking around the dining room on his two good legs, the blue book I longed to read useless in his hands. Someone came up the steps; one of my sisters, I thought, until the knock. Jasper opened the door to a little boy, who stepped in when I nodded.

"Charlie," Jasper said. "What in the world?"

"Nana sent me," the boy—Jasper's nephew—said importantly. His lovely face, wide at the cheekbones, narrow at the chin, with a perfectly shaped mouth and soft gray eyes, was much like his mother's. "She said you're to come home right away, they're holding dinner."

His eyes were fixed on my casts. "I'm Caroline," I offered. "You go to school with my little sisters, I think."

"Alice," he said, his face lighting up. "And Agnes, and Elaine." He inched closer. "Does it hurt? I heard the aeroplane *hit* you."

"An accident," I said, even as Jasper told Charlie not to pry.

THE NEXT TIME Jasper visited, I confessed to eavesdropping on him and Raney at the gazebo. Instead of being angry, he dropped the book (he was still pretending he came to read to me) and made a short, sharp noise resembling laughter. *Hak, hak.*

"I should have told you right away," I said. "I'm sorry."

"I might as well have kissed her on my front porch," he said.

"I'm the only one who saw."

"I wish," he said. "But my grandmother was out there, getting some air."

"How did I miss her?"

Jasper shrugged. "She tore me apart when I came back in. Couldn't I see that Raney was just toying with me, and why would I risk our family . . ."

"She thought of Raney as a risk?"

"Of course." He pinched the tip of his long nose between two fingers. "Too young for me, too flighty, no roots here in the village, bad enough for my reputation that she might damage my chances with someone from a family like mine."

Perhaps she'd spotted me lurking on the path. "I didn't even know you and Raney were seeing each other, until that night."

He traced a knot in the wooden floor with one foot and said, "She had a flair for keeping secrets. I thought she'd told you about us, though."

I shook my head. If I'd let myself understand, earlier, how much she'd hidden from me, I might not have seen her at all the weekend she met Jasper in the gazebo.

By then it was November and soon, before Thanksgiving but after our first dusting of snow, the doctor unwound the remaining bandages on my head. Agnes and Alice were out, and after Aunt Henrietta checked on Samuel, she and I studied what I had left and then began to experiment with the scissors. A fringe seemed like the best way to conceal the hairless patch where my scalp was gone, and my aunt cut a neat straight line, just touching my eyebrows. The rest she cut level with my earlobes, the way I've kept it ever since. I looked different, quite modern I thought, like the two women flyers who'd passed through town the previous year and startled everyone with their cropped hair. The ends swung when I leaned forward and hid my cheeks and part of my scar, while the fringe hid the worst part of my scalp.

I decided then that when I could get up, I'd wear what a flyer would wear: men's trousers (my aunt sometimes wore these in private, or when looking for specimens), boots, a big soft shirt, and a woolen jacket. My legs, which would be unsightly even when they began to work again, would be hidden. I wouldn't have to worry about which scars would show in a dress, or what a man might someday think as he removed that dress.

Jasper was so busy by then at the winery that he had to stop visiting in the afternoons, but he sent Adrien Hendricks to keep me company. He came as a favor to Jasper, not to me; they'd been friends since Adrien got to town and started working with Jasper's cousin. He might also have felt a twinge because he'd been one of Palmer and Elly's teachers. Since the end of the flying season, he'd been sanding propellers part-time at the factory, working off the cost of the hydro-aeroplane they were building for him and trying not to envy the companions who'd gone to San Diego or Florida for the winter.

Jasper had told him that I was interested in learning more about the flying school, but as he walked up to our house, he was mostly imagining what he'd do when he could ship his hydro-aeroplane home to Friesland, where he wouldn't be teasingly labeled the Flying Dutchman but would just be—himself, flying over the marshes to land on the dark violet surface of Lake Sneek. He might take off from the Zuyder Zee; in winter he might soar along the frozen canals as the skaters raced below. He was so deep in his daydreams, he'd tell me later, that when Alice and Agnes opened the door, he was surprised, in the corner of the dining room, by a white bier, a white vessel, a bed. A girl in the bed (that girl was me), white-faced with chopped dark hair and hyphenated eyebrows.

We've been close for so long now that I can't remember all we talked about that afternoon. Jasper, of course. My aunt, my sisters, what looked to him like a jar of dirt next to me (Samuel was hiding). Link's earlier adventures, which he knew lots about. During Link's race with Barney Oldfield, he'd tapped his wheels on the roof of Oldfield's car.

"Not," Adrien added, "that I'm blaming him for what happened to you. The newspapers were hard on him at first, but he was flying perfectly cautiously that day. The coroner's jury was fair when they ruled it an accident. But I figured you'd want to know more about the person who changed your life."

That he'd thought of that—that he grasped how much I longed

to know everything possible—made me like him. So did the fact that when I asked him why he'd really come, he looked steadily into my eyes and said, "I'd do *anything* for Jasper. Anything," in a way I didn't really understand, then. By the end of his visit I knew that although he'd enjoyed the quick fellowship of Mrs. Mackenzie's boardinghouse, the drunken mock duels and rowdy card games that cut through the different languages and occasional jealousies, his life too had been changed by an accident. His friend Kondo, who had clipped a windmill while practicing before a crowd of gaping farmers, was dead when they pulled him from the plane.

"So I know," Adrien said, "a little bit about how you feel."

He dreamed about Kondo, he said. And about how, if Jasper's family were different, he'd have taught Jasper to fly. After he left, I dreamed about Raney again. No one was hurt, no one was dead, Raney was wearing a blue-sprigged dress with wide sleeves, which as she walked calmly into the lake ballooned around her upper arms and caught the wind, keeping her afloat. She scudded across the water, one hand on her chest.

Through the winter Adrien kept visiting, finishing off the Amundsen with me and also telling me things about the flying school and making friends with Aunt Henrietta too. They went to some lectures; he showed her the machine he hoped to buy. She took him to search for fossils at the Glen. Just after Christmas, she arranged with my other teachers a schedule that would let me keep up until I could go back to school, and after that Adrien sometimes helped me study. I read everything I was supposed to and then, as my interests veered, other books that Adrien and Aunt Henrietta brought me.

In March, when I announced what I'd decided at the dinner table, my aunt did what she could to calm my parents. My mother said what she'd said for years, whenever Marion or I wanted to do something: "Who's going to help me with the little girls?"

"I'm not a little girl anymore," Elaine pointed out, reasonably. "I can take care of myself. I *do* take care of myself."

"Well," my mother said, waving one hand vaguely in the direction of the twins. "But them."

As Alice and Agnes looked at each other, exchanging one of their secret messages and then pretending interest in the carrots, my father pointed out that my long convalescence had already been hard on my mother.

"I know," I said. "If I could have done anything differently . . ."

"But you've been an excellent patient," Aunt Henrietta said calmly. Not a word about how much time she herself had spent caring for my sisters.

"Still," my father said.

It was cold that day, the wind leaking through the windows and the stove useless beyond the dining room. Aunt Henrietta pulled her skirt more closely around her legs and pointed out that I'd be done with school in just a few months. The best way for me to heal completely was to have some absorbing occupation.

"So she can break the rest of her bones?" my mother said. "So we can spend another half a year looking after her?"

"*Hester*," my father said sharply. From the expressions passing over the faces of my sisters during this exchange, a wise person might have guessed that only one of us would ever marry.

I TOOK ADVANTAGE of everyone. Where I should have been grateful for all the help I'd already been given, all the hours devoted to me—I took more, I took everything I could. I didn't have the money to enroll in the flying school, but when Adrien volunteered to teach me, I greedily accepted. What had Amundsen felt? I asked myself. Maybe this clarity, which had brought him so far. Although

Adrien's machine wasn't ready yet, he had access to several because of his work. We started late in April, when the strangers streaming in for the new session made us inconspicuous.

A friend of Jasper's let us use one of the battered school machines, which was parked in a hangar behind the shop awaiting some updated skids. Adrien, amazingly patient, went over the machine with me: upper plane, lower plane, forward elevating and deflecting planes, left and right stabilizing planes, rear rudder, bamboo frame. He taught me to check the wires running through the fairleads and over the pulleys; check the engine and all of the controls; check and double-check. With the lever between my legs and my shoulders in the yoke, we drilled for hours. Turn the wheel attached to the lever and feel the rudder move, pull the wheel and watch the elevating planes tilt up, push it away and see them tilt down. Lean right and left to feel the wires controlled by the yoke pull at the stabilizing planes. I'd prepared for this while my legs were healing, reading the same books the young men studied at the flying school. Now we were training my body to grasp what my mind had learned. The motions were more natural than I'd expected.

Jasper came by twice to watch, delighted that I was learning so quickly, but also, he admitted, jealous. A few days after his second visit, Adrien and three companions wheeled the machine down to Kingsley Flats. One man spun the propeller, the other two removed the blocks and let go of the frame. I rattled across the mud, kept on the ground by the wired-down throttle as Adrien called out instructions. Again and again, with the engine racketing behind me, I plowed across the bumpy field. My cheeks froze, my hands stiffened, but soon I got used to the noise and steady vibration behind me, the frame sticking out in front, the rattling all around. Adrien unwired the throttle and put on a different, smaller propeller, so I had full power but still couldn't take off. Then I did two more days of what, although the grass was still matted and just beginning to green, the men called grass-cutting. A little dance, training my feet on the throttle and brake; a new dance, easy to learn.

While I worked, the men from the shop tidied the shore, repairing the damage caused by the winter's ice and setting out ramps and turntables for the school. The thing, Adrien told me, was to hold the wheel lightly, surprisingly lightly, the way I'd hold my little sisters' hands. I needed to sense the movements of the front planes and the rudder, and if I gripped too hard, Adrien said, I wouldn't feel anything. His friends replaced my practice propeller with another, which let the wheels lift off when I was at full throttle but didn't have enough thrust to let me rise more than a few feet before I glided down.

Those were the first minutes I was off the ground, actually flying, and I knew right away that I loved it. My first hops were like my first minutes on a bicycle, that same startled reaction to every wobble and gust of wind, overcorrecting but then quieting, balancing easily and almost unconsciously as my body got used to the machine. And when Adrien turned me loose with the regular propeller, I was calm—almost calm—as I rose and kept on rising, soared the length of the field and out over the beach and the base of the lake, and then returned.

Each flight I went up higher, stayed up longer. Leaning into the turns happened naturally, it really was like riding a bike, and if I let my shoulders move as they wanted to move, then the turn came out perfectly. I made ellipses above the field, stretched them until I was far out over the lake, widened them to include the edge of the village. At last I saw what Link must have seen. No crowds, only a handful of friends—but the ground still sheeted away and the horizon dropped when I nosed up. I was passing a gull, I was next to a cloud. I was casting a shadow on the train and then over a patch of woods where the next Samuel hung upside down on a leaf, awaiting Aunt Henrietta.

Soon everything would turn upside down, as if the whole world had looped the loop. Flying schools would be training military pilots instead of sportsmen; Adrien would not be at the Zuyder Zee but at the naval aviation school at Pensacola; for a while I'd give flying lessons in San Antonio. Everything about flying would be different by the end of the war that, as I made my first flights, hadn't yet begun—but still, those first flights are what I dream about.

OPEN HOUSE

IN DECEMBER OF 1919, DAPHNE INVITED HENRIETTA TO join her on a visit to the Everglades, where she planned to study the natural history of the mangroves. Henrietta, who for years had longed to visit there, wasted an afternoon imagining how they'd tromp through the slick mud, investigating the sponges and bryozoans and barnacles growing on the roots—and then she pushed that vision firmly underwater. The Volstead Act had caused such upheaval around Crooked Lake that she didn't feel able to leave, especially not with Hester and Ambrose quarreling again. Ambrose had been sleeping above his shoe store since early summer, and Hester was more than usually despondent. Although Elaine, Agnes, and Alice were old enough now to look after themselves, they needed Henrietta in other ways, and she tried to spend time alone with each niece and to arrange pleasant outings. During the week between Christmas and New Year's, when the Durands held their open house, she brought Alice with her.

The big green house at the edge of the village still had all its porches then, along with the fanlight above the front door. The gazebo where Jasper had once kissed Raney stood at the back of the garden, across the path from the cliff; the fountain worked, the flagstones were level, the tools in the garden shed gleamed. The broad downstairs hall connected library to double parlor, dining room to kitchen to pantry: a useful arrangement for this gathering held each year to thank the Durands' employees and please their neighbors.

Afterwards a notice would appear in the *Gazette*. Who'd attended (half the village stopped by during the long hours of generous food and drink, along with people from vineyards and wineries around the lake). What was served, what the weather was like. *The elder Mrs. Durand*—Opal, as designated by the *Gazette*—*wearing an ink-blue dress and patent leather pumps, presided graciously as always, welcoming guests to the beautifully decorated reception rooms.*

The doors opened, opened, opened again—and there were the Perrottes, and Walter Fontaine, and three young men from the packing line at the winery. The fire flared each time. The ancient aunts, holding court in their special chairs, complained as they had for thirty years about the draft. In the early days, when Opal's sons were small and Nana, her mother-in-law, was strong and healthy, still handsome in the violet gowns she favored, she'd shown off her grandsons like a litter of prize pigs. Nearly twenty years later, when Didier returned from France with Chloe and their little boy, Nana had paraded Charlie from cousin to neighbor. Now Charlie was nearly grown and Nana refused to come downstairs. Still, Didier and Jasper had hung the wreaths and arranged the racks for the coats, suspended lanterns from the gazebo and the trees, tied back the drapes so the rooms could beckon to the street.

Or maybe, Opal thought, watching the delivery truck move slowly past, so that anyone who'd decided to skip the event could be seen. *As evening fell, the rooms brightly signaled all passers-by, promising good cheer and good company.* No one could afford to offend her family. Crates of extra glasses migrated up to the house from the winery just for this, and she'd hired several of the girls who did seasonal work in the vineyards. Two were clearing the coffee things now and returning with platters of savory canapés. Later the drinks and hors d'oeuvres would be replaced by a big buffet and then by dessert, ending finally with brandy and wine.

So many hours still to go. So many conversations. If she'd worn her gray pumps, her feet wouldn't be so sore. If she turned this all over to Chloe, if she could take Didier aside and say—

She spoke to a neighbor and two of her daughters; to the man who ran the pharmacy and an acquaintance from Oneonta. Bernard came over to thank her for piling the apples on one of his decorative platters, and she told him how much she loved the grass-green lizard skirting the rim. She greeted four vineyard owners from Bully Hill, who were talking glumly with some growers from the valley, and then she refilled the punch cups of two high school boys. Friends of Charlie's? In the hall, snow boots leaned against each other on the metal trays, and ridges of hats and mittens snaked along the bench. The backyard, visible through the long parlor windows, looked exactly as it was meant to, the deep unbroken snow shining beneath the lanterns, the gazebo as stark as if it were carved in ice, the dark trees beyond the light suggesting miles of mysterious woods.

The door opened again—Henrietta Atkins, with her niece Alice, windblown and red-cheeked—and outside the trees swayed. "We snowshoed down from my house," Henrietta announced. "We saw wild turkeys!" Alice added.

From her place near the Christmas tree, Chloe listened with what, for a moment, looked to Opal like envy. And from the dining room—had he been watching out the window for them to arrive?— her floppy-haired, long-fingered grandson Charlie bounded across the hall, knocking down boots like bowling pins as he rushed toward the new arrivals.

THE TEDIOUS GARAGE owner caught Charlie near Nana's favorite sofa. His buildings, his automobiles, the difficulties of finding a new mechanic—what was Charlie planning to do after graduation? Was he interested in engine repair? His chin mole wagged with his words. Alice and Miss Atkins were less than twenty feet away, his teacher so oddly dressed that Charlie hardly recognized her. At school she wore white blouses and dark skirts, practical clothes that wouldn't catch on a microscope or brush the flame of a Bunsen burner, but tonight she'd celebrated with a scarlet dress lumpily tiered from hip to calf and frilled around the low neck. Old-fashioned, like something his grandmother might have worn when he was a boy. Or maybe just old—Alice had told him that her aunt bought clothes at the church jumble sale.

"Would you excuse me?" he said. "I have to talk to my teacher." A few strides and he was there, trying not to look at the freckled slice of chest revealed by Miss Atkins's dress.

"Aren't I ridiculous?" she said gaily, pointing down. At least she wasn't wearing pants. "I forgot to bring shoes." She wiggled her toes, clad only in stockings—but the next toes over, demure in black ribbed cotton, were what made him blush. "Alice left hers behind too."

With an effort Charlie looked up and complimented Alice's dress.

"It used to be Caroline's," Alice said, spreading the skirt. Surely the dress had never looked so good on her sister. The warm deep brown set off Alice's hair, which she'd done differently, one pale band on either side pulled back and plaited. He wished he'd been the one to plait it.

"We were working on a terrarium," Miss Atkins continued. "We lost track of the time. When we realized how late it had gotten, we threw on our boots and snowshoes and forgot we'd left our shoes

behind." He forced his attention back to her. "Have you heard anything more from our friend in Pennsylvania?"

Charlie shook his head. "Not yet," he said, trying to match her
cheerful tone. Enough gloom in the house already. Many of the wineries were already shuttered; others would be locked by officials on
January 16th, when the new laws went into effect. Only a few had
managed to make other arrangements. One friend's family had gotten a permit to make and sell medicinal wine, to be prescribed by
doctors, while his own family's winery had a contract for sacramental wine. A rabbi in Rochester needed a supplier of kosher wine,
too: a sign, his father promised, that not everything would collapse.
But Charlie wasn't sure he believed him. In the last few months his
father had begun to look like he slept beneath a sofa, and even now,
greeting guests by one of Bernard's famous carp-handled vases, he
was frowning.

At him? Maybe because he was talking with Miss Atkins. His
father thought she interfered: Miss Atkins, who cared mainly about
fish and fossils and moths and bees, her students—she'd been teaching for more than forty years—and now him. He said, quietly, "I
wrote Professor Hardiman again, as you suggested. Just to remind
him I'm interested."

It was wonderful that she thought so highly of him. Yet possibly
mortifying: What if she was wrong? She probably *was* wrong. A bud-
ding paleontologist, she'd proclaimed, after he'd done no more than
go on a few field trips, examine some fossils, research their background in a couple of libraries. Based on that, and on some drawings
he'd made and a few notes he'd written, she'd begun lending him
her own books and ordering others from Cornell. Then, without
even asking him, she'd written on his behalf to her old friend at the
University of Pennsylvania.

It had been thrilling when Professor Hardiman contacted him—

but he'd also felt like a fraud. Couldn't anyone see who he was? The best student of an elderly high school teacher from a village in the middle of nowhere. *We'd be delighted to consider you for admission next year*: this, from a man who, even if he was as old as Miss Atkins, had once been to the Bridger Basin and explored the Niobrara Chalk, uncovered bones of the *Elasmosaurus* and the gigantic *Camerasaurus*, worked among the skulls and talons and boxes of bones. The professor wrote that vast amounts of material came into his laboratory from the expeditions of former students and friends, and that Charles (he called him Charles, which instantly made Charlie feel more serious) might be able to join such an expedition, even as a freshman.

That had been encouraging, and although his father argued for Cornell—so much closer, which mattered in more ways than his father knew—and his mother for Yale, he'd nearly decided to go to Penn on the basis of that one letter. He wrote back promptly, saying he was free after his graduation at the end of June—and then the professor didn't write back. And didn't write back, and didn't write back.

"Why don't I write him myself, and see what's happening," Miss Atkins said. "I expect something came up for him at work." As she spoke, Charlie's uncle materialized behind her. "Jasper!" she said happily.

"You look very festive," he said, bending to kiss her cheek. "As do you, young Alice." At his elbow a man Charlie recognized as the new chemist at the winery nodded at all of them. "What word of Caroline?"

"She's thinking of coming back east," Miss Atkins said. "Some flying school on Long Island caught her eye, but there's another in Florida—she still isn't sure."

The front door opened again; an ornament fell off the tree. As

Jasper listened to Miss Atkins's speculations about Alice's older sister, Charlie, seeing an opening, moved toward Alice. But before he
could reach her, his uncle turned and intercepted him.

"Have you been upstairs?" Jasper said.

Charlie shook his head, hoping Alice would stay put. Already
the three Vandenberg sisters, red-haired and freckled, were moving
intently her way.

"It's a while since anyone's visited Nana," Jasper said. "Why don't
you bring your great-grandmother a few things to nibble on, and a
glass of wine?" Obedient, for the moment, Charlie headed upstairs.

EARLIER, BEFORE ALICE had arrived to help her with the terrarium, Henrietta had sifted carefully through the shelves of her extra
closet before settling at last on the wonderful old red dress. She knew
the color didn't suit her complexion, that the cut emphasized her
bony chest and did nothing for her shape—but she liked trying to
imagine how the woman who'd once loved it had felt. Vivid, perhaps
a touch scandalous. Proud of her . . . dark hair, Henrietta decided,
masses of very dark hair. Against her own gray it was at least cheerful, which everyone needed this year, and just silly enough to render
her intellectually invisible. In the dress she was a foolish old woman,
safe enough for anyone to talk to.

Now, disguised as a mobile Christmas ornament, she watched
Charlie return from his errand upstairs and then, with his uncle Jasper, work together to charm Mrs. McCallum out of her bad mood.
Of all her students, even including Bernard with his remarkable
bowls and platters, Charlie was the best. Not the quickest but the
most insightful, able to see deeply into problems and make connections. He could spend a whole day collecting samples and then study
far into the night when that was needed, and while anyone would

know him as a Durand—he shared with his uncle his blocky figure, his long pointed nose, and excellent manners—he still surprised her. Unlike his father and uncle, he seemed to value his gifts very little.

"How is Jeffrey doing?" she heard Charlie ask.

Instantly Mrs. McCallum brightened. Her son was *so* much better, she said; he was staying in Miami with two friends from his former platoon, planning to breed horses for the track. Charlie smiled and Jasper offered a story about another friend, also recovering well from a wound he'd gotten in France. No one mentioned the men from the village—all of them Henrietta's former students—who'd been killed, or died of the influenza, or been wounded so badly they were still in hospitals far away. For a minute the room dimmed as she remembered Izzy, returning from the Civil War so many years ago. One hand missing, the other crippled, and his mind crippled too: how young she'd been (how grown-up she'd felt) when, coming home from school, she'd spied on him and the other wounded veterans sitting in the square! Astonishing that she'd lived long enough to witness another group of shattered men, another party where guests talked about anything but those men. About, now, how relatively fortunate Jeffrey had been; how long it had taken—was still taking—for men to find work. By the time they were done, Mrs. McCallum looked almost happy. Charlie shared that social ease with most of his family but didn't seem to grasp that his intellectual gifts were his alone.

What he wanted, he'd told her, was to be *useful*. To his family, to his community, even to the larger world—and in that context, what use was a brilliant eye for grasping the structure and meaning of the natural world, or for being able to intuit almost instantly, from a few inches of fossilized bone, what creature it might have belonged to, and how that creature might have lived? What good was solitary work? She hadn't mentioned his hesitations in her letter to Benjamin Hardiman, speaking instead about Charlie's unusual intuitions. She'd noted his rare lack of defensiveness and his ability to accept criticism easily, which made it possible for him to learn almost anything. What she'd wanted to say, but (wisely, she thought now) kept to herself, was: *He reminds me of you.* Not present-day Benjamin; they hadn't seen each other for years. But Benjamin as he'd been during the biology course they'd taken one summer more than forty years ago, on an island off the New Bedford coast.

Their friendship rested almost entirely on those long days of collecting and dissecting, the hours of lectures and the passionate discussions afterwards. Most of her closest friends were, like Daphne, those who'd warmed their backs against the same giant rock, watched the same teachers drawing coelenterates on the board. Although some of her companions had gone on to be famous scientists, leading this university or that museum, while others, like Benjamin, had settled into smaller departments, most had stayed in touch and tried to help each other.

And Benjamin had responded kindly to her letter, welcoming Charlie as a prospect for his program at the university. How puzzling that since then he'd ignored Charlie's replies. After Charlie's second letter too had gone unanswered, she'd secretly written again. He'd answered promptly.

I'm not sure what to tell you: when I contacted a friend in Doylestown to see about placing Charles on an expedition this summer, he simply didn't answer me. Edward and I have been out of touch recently but I felt perfectly comfortable asking him to help your protégé. You and I haven't seen each other in far longer, but even if I had to refuse you something, I would never do it this way. I remind myself that two years ago he lost his only son in the war; of course this has changed him—but still. Let me see what I can arrange elsewhere.

But still he hadn't written Charlie. Maybe she'd worn out his goodwill? Across the room, the fire flared as someone rearranged the logs, and Leon, the head of the family, in a faded vest that made her appreciate again her festive red, moved from guest to guest with two open bottles of some special vintage. When she was—twelve, perhaps? The age when she used to see Izzy; her hair in braids, like Alice's; her teacher drawing a map of Brazil on the board—she'd seen from her seat near the window a beautifully dressed little boy being walked by his even more beautifully dressed mother to his first day of school: Leon at the age of five or six, a little prince. Over the years, as he doubled the size of the winery, he'd expanded similarly and assumed an almost comic dignity. Now all he'd made of the family business was threatened.

Charlie's father, Didier, stopped near her elbow—accidentally, she thought; Mrs. Couperin had turned into his path as he'd tried to glide by—and she braced herself.

"I wondered when you might grace us with your presence," he said. He gestured toward the table, where the appetizers were making room for great platters of turkey and ham. "Won't you have some supper?"

"Soon," she said. Another of her former students emerged from the kitchen balancing two big ovals along each arm: how graceful she was, and how strong! Miranda, carrying carrots. And holding the door open for her was Bernard, who'd been teaching Charlie some of the techniques he used to make casts of bones, seedpods, even live animals for his plates and vessels. She reminded herself to ask if he'd visit her classes next year.

She smiled at Bernard over Didier's shoulder and then, since Didier said nothing, complimented the table decorations. "I wanted to say hello to your grandmother," she continued. "Do you know where she is?"

"Upstairs," Didier said. "Sulking. I don't know what else to call it."

That strong-willed woman, sulking: she hadn't expected that. Diplomatically, she said, "It's a hard time for everyone."

"No one's thrilled to be doing this," he said. "But after last year—we had to make the effort."

They'd skipped the open house last year, Henrietta remembered. The worst wave of the influenza had passed by then, but everyone had been exhausted and grieving. Both schools had closed, the movie theater, most of the businesses. Even the celebrations for the Armistice had been muted. Two of her former students who'd joined up had died of influenza in their camps. And in France two had been killed in action and five had been wounded. Out of respect for them (and perhaps a kind of guilt: Didier and Jasper had been too old to serve and Charlie too young), the Durands had canceled the usual celebration.

"It's a lovely spread this year," Henrietta said. She felt Didier's gaze drop, as if her platitudes embarrassed him, and then snag on the froth of dyed chiffon at her neck.

"Chloe does most of it," he said, when he looked up again. "A shame your friend Miss Bannister couldn't be here. Are you working on something new together?"

"Daphne is always working on something," Henrietta said blandly, ignoring his interest in her relationship with Daphne. "As am I. Charlie seems excited about the possibility of studying in Philadelphia."

"Your idea, I gather," Didier said.

She said something vague, meant to mollify, about the university's strong paleontology department and her illustrious friend.

"But there are excellent paleontologists at Yale, and at Cornell. So why would you push Charlie toward Penn?"

"Because that's where I know someone. I want to make sure he's looked after, I suppose." She paused, hearing again the word "push," trying to understand Didier's edgy tone. He didn't seem to like it when Charlie worked at Bernard's pottery, either. "Didn't you spend some time in Pennsylvania, when you were Charlie's age?"

"I was older," he said, straightening his cuffs. "But yes—that's where I met Chloe."

"I'd forgotten," Henrietta said, still puzzled by his tone. "I just remember you being away for a couple of years, and then coming back from France with Chloe and Charlie."

Didier frowned and scratched at an invisible speck on one cuff.

"Did I do something wrong?" Henrietta asked. "I recommend students to programs all the time." *Even you*, she added silently, remembering the letter she'd written for him when he went to college. He hadn't been so stuffy as a boy. "Charlie's a remarkable student. I was trying to make sure he had as many opportunities as possible."

"Indeed," Didier said. He looked down at the crook of his elbow, where a hand suddenly appeared. "Chloe," he said, as his wife slid in beside him. "Henrietta and I were just talking about Charlie's prospects."

Her eyes, Henrietta thought, were as striking as ever. Wide, slightly protuberant, the gray irises flecked with amber and the outer corners unusually open. Charlie had inherited not only her eyes but the shape of her face, wide at the cheekbones, narrow at the chin. Her steady regard felt like a metal blade sliding over Henrietta's skin.

"Do we have prospects?" Chloe said. "Any of us? Charlie might be better off looking for paying work. Your job"—she was still looking at Henrietta—"is at least secure, people always need teachers. But the rest of us—who's going to survive this? Who's going to still be here, in five years? Or twenty?"

"We'll be fine," Didier said. "You know I'm doing everything I can."

"Fine," she said. "If anyone thinks of a way out of this, it will be Jasper. Or maybe Charlie: unless Henrietta succeeds in sending him away. Or unless her little niece turns his head completely."

"Alice?" Henrietta said, shocked at Chloe's bitterness.

"Alice," Chloe repeated. "Isn't that why you're encouraging him to go so far away to school? Although I'm sure I can't imagine how we'll pay for it."

Almost accidentally, Henrietta gestured at the warmly lit and fragrant room, overflowing with guests.

"Should we act as if the business *isn't* still thriving?" Chloe said.

Once, Henrietta remembered, not long after Didier had brought Chloe and Charlie home, she'd found Chloe sitting by herself on one of the docks, disconsolately watching the *Penn Yan* steam away. She'd been crying, but when Henrietta asked if she could help, Chloe's face went blank. Now she erased her expression again as Charlie and Alice bumped into Didier, who tugged his elbow away from her hand.

"There you are," Didier said to his son.

He spun Charlie ninety degrees, until he was facing the kitchen door. Alice, as if yoked to him, spun too. "Could you see if the girls in the kitchen need any help?"

CHASED UPSTAIRS EARLIER, now to the back of the house: no one seemed to want him in the thick of the party, which since he'd found Alice was fine with Charlie. He walked straight through the kitchen with her at his side, ignoring the sink filled with cooking pans and the two young women bent over the pies. When he reached the back door, which was set at a right angle to the door to the cellar stairs, he opened one with either hand before whistling into the yard. Then he stepped back, using his body to channel the flying gray shapes down the stairwell.

Alice fit herself next to the doorframe and touched the dogs as they passed. "Olive!" she said. "Oscar!" Bearded, wiry-haired, with tufts around their eyes and fluffy paws: descendants of those his father claimed to have brought back across the ocean. He couldn't remember either that trip or the family vineyard in France, and the breed's fancy name had disappeared by the time he could talk. Here, people called them "the French dogs" and cursed their fence-jumping skills. All over town, mutts bore tufty heads and beards, wiry gray patches on their chests, or, sometimes, just the gigantic hairy feet. This pair, looking much like their ancestors, pounded off in search of mice.

He and Alice followed more slowly. "Can I show you something?" he asked.

"Anything," she said. He loved her fearlessness. Although she was two years behind him in school, she knew more about almost everything and she never minded getting dirty or wet. She'd walk up a creek bed, scale a gritty cliff, reach into a hollow tree just to see what might be hiding. Once, when they'd found a mummified bat, she'd stroked the fur on its back against her cheek.

"Careful," he said, steering her past the boiler. He pulled at a dirty string and the big room lit up, revealing the freshly built wall.

"Is that new?"

He nodded. The wall stretched across the house, separating off the back third of the basement and pierced by one big door awaiting a padlock but for now simply closed. Charlie lifted the hasp bar from the eye and showed Alice the new storage rooms lined along the narrow corridor. Each room had its own door, ajar for now, and each was labeled. *Nana. Sylvie & Madeleine & Clementine. Leon & Opal.*

Jasper. Didier & Chloe. No label for him; he was too young. But for everyone else an enormous locker, smelling of wood, lined with shelves and dividers. Tidy lists hung inside the doors: how many cases of champagne, sherry, reds and whites from this vintage or that stockpiled for each person. Sawdust still marked the floors, and here and there lay the dollies used to wheel in the crates. Soon these doors would be padlocked too.

"So *much*," Alice said. "It looks like a warehouse."

"Doesn't it?" Charlie said. "But no one knows how long this will last—years, probably—and when they were sitting around the table, calculating so many bottles a week, times so many weeks in a year . . . it got to be a lot pretty quickly. Plus one party like this"— he pointed at the ceiling—"is a whole stack of cases. Did your family stock up?"

Alice laughed. "A few bottles of whiskey. I think Aunt Henrietta bought a case of wine. She's so clever, though—I bet she'll start making her own."

"It's not illegal," Charlie said. "Any more than this is." He gestured at the row of little rooms. "But it's strange when you see all the bottles together."

The gallon of clear liquid they found in Jasper's locker made Charlie laugh: grape brandy, he said. Fantastically strong, for fortifying the wine. For a while after they found that, they stood chatting easily, watching the dogs weave through the storage rooms. Oscar jammed his snout under Nana's lowest shelf and emerged with his beard and eye tufts heavily coated with sawdust. Olive's paws turned white. When they were puppies, Charlie remembered, before their backs had darkened to gray, they'd been that pale all over. Their heads, now a warm brown, had been closer to fawn. Olive scrabbled under a shelf and fished out a wad of paper, which she batted his way.

Alice tossed the crumpled paper across the floor so that Olive could retrieve it. She held out her hand and Olive dropped the ball of paper into it proudly. Turning toward Oscar, who was rooting around in the room marked with Charlie's parents' names, Alice said, "They haven't stored up nearly as much as your uncle."

"Maybe my father thinks he'll figure something out later?" Charlie said.

She tossed the paper again for Olive. "What does he think about you going to Philadelphia?"

"What do *you* think about it?"

They'd spent far more time together than most people understood—largely because her mother was so often sick, so overwhelmed and careless, that she let Alice go off alone with him. That, and the fact that Miss Atkins trusted him completely.

Alice, instead of answering him, crouched down and scratched Oscar's ears, which brought Olive over. Charlie moved closer to Alice, with the excuse of pushing Olive's nose gently away from Oscar's head.

"My aunt really wants you to go," she said.

"Your aunt," Charlie started to say. Then he caught himself. "The professor she put me in touch with seemed very welcoming at first. But now—he hasn't written me back, and I think he doesn't want me after all. And anyway—"

He took a deep breath and slid his hand from Olive's head to Oscar's, which was covered by Alice's hand. "I don't know that I want to be so far away from home. From you. There's a good program at Cornell."

"Cornell's not far," Alice said calmly. Then she turned her hand over on Oscar's head, so that her palm faced Charlie's. Oscar stood still, his head warm, the tufts of hair at the base of his ears tickling the side of Charlie's hand. Olive, beside him, politely bumped his other elbow but somehow knew not to insist.

He couldn't sort out what he felt. The dogs were breathing, Alice was breathing, their hands were touching. Above them feet moved forward and back. Above them the door to the basement opened and his father called impatiently, "Charlie? Are you down there?"

AS A BOY, Didier had been obedient to a fault, studying what his parents suggested, paying attention to the intricacies of the family business as soon as Leon thought he was ready. What an earnest little student! Even his boots had been perfectly, tidily laced. From the time he was ten, he'd known he was expected to take over the winery. He spent afternoons in the office, studying accounting and marketing, and because he was handy mechanically he also apprenticed briefly in the different departments, where, although the foremen knew he was only sampling what for them were their lives, they worked him hard. At his father's suggestion he studied industrial engineering in college, with an eye toward modernizing the plant. Right after graduation, and with his father's blessing, he took a one-year position at a tile works in Pennsylvania. An excellent way, they both thought, for him to broaden his knowledge of factory management.

Now, when Didier tried to imagine the young man who'd set off for Doylestown, he saw him as if through the bottom of a basket. Tiny glimpses, brightly lit, the rest blocked by strips of cane. He'd known nothing about himself, and almost as little about anyone else. He had no sense of why the workmen resented his endlessly observing eye or the drawings he made of their tasks. And when he gathered up his sketches and equipment and left the plant for his room—he was lodging in his employer's house—he seemed to leave everything rational behind and cross over into a dream.

The house was somewhere between a castle and a hive, entirely made of poured concrete with hardly a straight edge anywhere. Rooms with curved walls and vaulted ceilings led haphazardly to other rooms by way of a few steps down, a few more up, the walls embedded with tiles and pottery collected from all over the world. His room, which was shaped like a teepee, was on what would have been the third floor, had the rooms separated neatly into levels: high in the air, facing the tile works. At his desk, a concrete slab that flowed directly out of the wall, he was meant to be calculating what new equipment Mr. Hazelius might need, how to install it, how best to train the workmen to use it. Instead he found himself eavesdropping on the complicated life of the house. Maids, a cook, a driver, an elderly man who announced himself as an archivist. Mr. Hazelius's son, Edward, who was near his own age and was apparently being groomed to take over the tile works. With his young wife and their little boy, Edward sat for hours on the patio below Didier's window, sometimes with his father but more often—Mr. Hazelius traveled a great deal—with his friend and neighbor, a man named Miles Fairchild. Both had gone to Penn but Edward hadn't finished his degree. He was dreamy, Didier learned. Prone to odd enthusiasms, utterly bored by the tile works. His passion was the excavation of fossil bones, and he'd traveled with Miles in Kansas and Nebraska, digging up the bones of creatures Didier had never heard of. He realized, listening to their conversations during his first weeks, that they were preparing for a trip.

Certain scenes from that summer remained in Didier's memory as clearly as the drawings he made in the factory. What he couldn't recover were the feelings or how he'd rationalized what he'd done. He'd been twenty-one. Edward's wife was equally young. He had no idea what had gone wrong between Chloe and Edward, but he could see how useless Edward was at the tile works. A few days after Edward left with his friend, the little boy, Lawrence, developed mumps, and he and Chloe both disappeared for nearly two weeks. Another week passed before Didier spotted the boy playing in his usual place in the walled garden. Not long after that, he began running into Chloe everywhere.

Or that was how he remembered it now—had she really started appearing on the path between the row of tulip trees just as he walked back from the plant, on the patio before he went in to breakfast? Or had he simply become more aware of her?

It was like being shot. Like being knocked down by an automobile. Like waking up to find that everything he'd thought of as himself had disappeared and nothing was left but a single want: to be with Chloe, Chloe, Chloe. There was no part of the weeks that followed that he could bear, now, to recollect: especially not discovering she was pregnant, or when, after Edward got back, she did what she needed to do to make sure that Edward could believe the baby was his. The months that followed had been so difficult that he couldn't understand, then or now, how he'd survived them. He kept working, he stayed in the house, he acted around Edward's father, around Edward and Chloe, as if nothing had changed. As if—Chloe had begged him to do this—he were simply an employee. He learned, then, how devious he could be. How smoothly he could say one thing and mean another, not a muscle twitching on his face.

The baby was born in May. Not long afterwards, Chloe came to his room late at night and told him she couldn't live without him; she'd told Edward everything. Two days later, after scenes he'd managed to block almost completely from his memory, they left.

He booked a suite on the ship for "Mr. and Mrs. Durand and son Charles," which was how they arrived in France. For several months they traveled to places where no one knew them, finally coming to rest at his relatives' vineyard and winery in the Loire Valley. No one questioned him when he presented Chloe and baby Charles as his wife and son. They welcomed him into the business and helped him rent a house; they gave him the dogs that seemed to ratify his family as a family. Two years later, when he returned with that family to Crooked Lake, he told everyone that he and Chloe had married secretly in Doylestown, and that Charlie had been born there just before they all went to France.

Inevitably, though, he'd had to confess the truth to his parents: that Chloe's divorce was still hypothetical, and that Charles, although his biological son—he could still feel the depth of his blush when he'd said this—was legally Edward Hazelius's son. It took years, and all his father's considerable resources, to work through the legal details. A judge in Pennsylvania had facilitated the divorce, which fortunately Edward by then also wanted. Several lawyers in New York, and another judge, had worked to marry them quietly and arrange his legal adoption of Charlie. So much time, so much money, so many favors granted—and still, he and Chloe had to invent a past for her suspended on a few unhelpful points. They mentioned her dead father and her elderly mother while erasing other relatives; invented a party where they'd supposedly met; and swore, as if this were part of their marriage vows, never to mention her first son, Lawrence. Only his parents knew he existed. Not until his own son began to walk and speak did Didier begin to understand what they'd done in leaving him.

"Edward will let me go," Chloe had told him on the bench beneath the copper beech. Weeping, weeping. "But only if I leave Lawrence. 'You go,' he said. 'He stays. For good. You don't see him, you don't write him, you don't ask for news of him. You give him up.'"

"What kind of a person—" Didier had asked, holding her.

"I think his father's behind it," she said. Edward's father, his employer. "He was always against me. He tried to keep us from getting married, he threatened to cut Edward off when we did—now I'm just behaving as he always thought I would."

Not all those scenes moved through Didier's mind at the open house—but some did, especially after he sent Charlie to the kitchen only to have him disappear, and as he began to suspect where Charlie was, and with whom. He forced himself to move through the rooms, briefly joining different conversations; easy enough, since everyone had read the same newspaper article, clarifying exactly what would be legal after midnight on January 16th. *You may drink intoxicating liquor in your own home or in the home of a friend when you are a bona fide guest. You may buy intoxicating liquor on a bona fide medical prescription of a doctor. A pint can be bought every ten days. You may keep liquor in any storage room or club locker, provided the storage place is for the exclusive use of yourself, family, or bona fide friends. You may manufacture, sell or transport liquor for non-beverage or sacramental purposes provided you obtain a Government permit.*

All the things a person couldn't do followed—but he tried to stay focused on those first lines, by which he hoped to keep his family afloat. He could sell off some of his stock as sacramental wine. He could press and sell grape juice, which meant he'd be buying at least some grapes, which meant a few vineyards could keep going. Some vineyards planned to sell grapes to households wanting to make their legal allotment of wine; he had ideas about concentrating the juice, or possibly dehydrating it. Jasper was looking into making tartaric acid cheaply from the grape skins, which could be sold to manufacturers of baking powder.

The kitchen door opened, pushed by the hip of a girl carrying a platter. Not Charlie but his dogs rushed past her legs, dashing between and around a thicket of other legs. Someone squealed. "Olive!" he called sharply. "Oscar! Sit."

They sat: as obedient, despite their size and general untidiness, as he'd once been. Where was Charlie? He turned as the kitchen door opened again, but this time Chloe came through, pointing at the clock—past eight, he saw—and rounding up volunteers to finish clearing the platters of turkey and ham and potatoes. Behind her, his mother was supervising the final touches to the bowls of trifle and the bourbon-soaked cake, the pies and the floating island.

"I lost track of him," he said, when Chloe came over to ask if he'd seen Charlie. "But I think he's somewhere with Alice." Her eyes, which when he let himself really see them were still, after eighteen years and all that had happened, capable of making him feel like he'd toppled slowly into cool water, closed briefly and then fixed on his.

"We should . . ." she said.

"I know," he said. "I know."

"But I don't think sending him off to Philadelphia is the answer either. I wish Henrietta hadn't interfered like that."

"He won't go to Philadelphia," Didier said.

Her eyes, again. "How do you know?"

He felt calmer now. Quite calm. "I just do," he said. "That's not going to work out for him." Then he moved to help his mother, who was bringing from the kitchen a giant glass bowl filled with custard and cake and jam. The bowl, faceted and silver-rimmed, hid her entire chest, and for just a minute her head seemed to float above a glass bosom.

THE DOOR OPENED, opened again, and Didier's mother, after depositing the glittering bowl with Didier, greeted a friend who after

the Armistice had stayed on in France and attended a school organized to keep American soldiers occupied while they waited to be
shipped back home. His had been a farm school; he had learned
about French crops and soils and methods. Not as much as Didier
had learned during his stay there, which they'd always presented
to outsiders as a carefully designed apprenticeship with the French
wing of the family.

He was walking, now, her complicated oldest son, from the back
of the dining room toward the front door, his hand held out to greet
a group of men from the packing room, his face as cheerful and welcoming as it had always been and would be into old age unless some
other crack appeared in his wife's polished performance. Perhaps it
would happen tonight. After the last of the trifle had been scraped
into bowls, after the older men had finished their final brandies, he
would ease them out to the porch and help organize the cleaning up.
Then the bedrooms would fill, one by one, and the doors would close.

Didier and Chloe would be the last awake and Didier would
finally close their door too and lie down next to Chloe, his thick,
strong body so obviously still her great delight. His hands would
reach for her. Afterwards, she might confess—what was it she'd
done, or said? At night Opal had lain in bed down the hall, trying
to imagine Chloe in Doylestown and the moment when she moved
on Didier. And then she'd buried the vision: her family depended on
accepting the mother of her only grandchild. Jasper had failed them;
to Chloe, who although she couldn't produce another child had at
least given them Charlie, they owed everything.

What bad luck, then, that Henrietta Atkins had encouraged
Charlie's interest in fossils! At first the little brachiopods and gas-
tropods he brought home from the Glen had seemed harmless; all
Henrietta's students went on those field trips, and both Didier and
Jasper remembered handling the mysterious shapes with pleasure.

But then Henrietta had gotten Charlie interested in the fossil mammals collected by Leidy and Cope, and after that in dinosaurs. The way Henrietta pushed this material back into their lives felt almost malicious, as if she knew Didier's secrets. As if she'd read the first letters he'd sent home from the tile works, describing the fairy-tale house and his employer's son's passion for dinosaur bones. Because of her, they all spun their wineglasses at dinner while Charlie talked about dinosaurs, fossil formation in wet and dry climates, his friend Bernard's experiments with casts and imprints. It was hard not to imagine, during those painful moments, what Charlie's life would have been like if Chloe had stayed where she belonged.

Opal rearranged the candlesticks and then strode to the archway leading into the dining room, where Alice, bent at the waist, was holding the dogs by their collars. Charlie, usefully, was nowhere in sight, and for a couple of minutes Opal made small talk about the dogs and the various adventures of Alice's sisters.

She kept her tone bright, polite—which, she knew, intimidated many girls—before asking directly, "What do you think about Charlie's plans for next year?"

"I think whatever he does, he'll do well at it," Alice said. Her eyes, fixed on the dogs, were hidden from Opal.

"Charlie is wonderful at everything, isn't he?"

"Everything," Alice agreed.

"He's like his father that way," Opal said. "I imagine you wish he'd stay closer to home."

"Whatever he does is fine," Alice said.

"But you're fond of him," Opal insisted.

Alice, scratching under Olive's collar, said, "We've been friends since we were tiny."

"That's true of most of his friends, isn't it?" Opal said thoughtfully. "But one of his gifts, I've always thought, is his way of making each person think he or she is his *best* friend. It's a bit deceitful, since he can't be best friends with everyone—but still it's charming. You probably think he's closer to you than to anyone else."

Alice whispered something to the dogs and then released them. They darted toward the kitchen as she straightened. "Charming?" she said. "He must get that from you."

Opal stared at the girl's stocking feet: she might have been ten; she should have been harmless.

"You'll need that locker downstairs," Alice added. She left, presenting Opal with her slim, straight back, her simple braid.

MOST OF THE guests were gone by the time Henrietta let the clamoring dogs through the kitchen door. She was ready to go as well and had already put on her coat and her boots, but then Jasper's friend Leo Marburg, the chemist the Durands had hired just before everything collapsed, had started talking to her as he buckled his own boots, and when Jasper offered them both a last drink only to find that the bottle had disappeared, they'd followed him into the kitchen. As the dogs streaked across the snowy yard and circled the gazebo, she learned that Leo had rented a place in town—a cottage, in a pleasant grove of hazel trees.

"I'm glad you found something," she said. Behind her the dogs stopped, sniffed, and crossed the path behind the gazebo, poking at the base of the whitened cliff. "But I hate that so many people have already sold up and left town."

Leo shrugged. "It's bad for people who've always lived here," he said, pushing his hair back with a thin hand. He'd been sick for a long time, she knew. But he seemed fine now. "Not so bad, though, for those of us new to town."

Jasper, unable to find the brandy, poured sherry into three

delicate glasses and then pointed toward the panes in the door. "What," he said, "are they doing out there?"

The snowy garden, still lit by the lanterns hanging from the trees and the gazebo, gleamed like a frozen lake but seemed to be empty until two gray shapes dashed along the base of the cliff in the direction of the shore. They stopped abruptly, barked, and then reversed, this time bolting back toward the winery.

"Those dogs have cornered something," Leo observed. "Shall we try to help?"

Jasper grabbed a coat and boots while she and Leo slogged into the garden. She let Leo go first; the snow was up to her knees. By the time they reached the gazebo the dogs had vanished, and Henrietta and Leo stopped and waited for Jasper.

"What was *that* about?" Jasper said when he reached them. He batted snow from one of the benches and sat down. "Charlie's dogs—I wish they were as well behaved as he is."

"What is he up to this summer?" Leo asked.

Jasper gestured toward Henrietta, who sat beside him. The moon was high and nearly full; when she held out her arm, it cast one shadow from the lantern on the lattice behind her and another, brighter, from the light of the moon.

"It's not up to me," Henrietta said. "I don't know what he'll decide to do."

"If he's not busy," Leo said, "Jasper and I have some ideas we thought might interest him. It's a lot of work, we need the help. And he's so smart—well, you know."

He glanced at Jasper, who kept an eye out for the dogs but also chimed in as they described their plan. Didier had reorganized the facilities to make and sell grape juice—but they wanted to do something different, pressing grape types separately and bottling the pure juice, with different labels, as "wine juice." Burgundy-type and porttype, sauterne-type and Riesling-type: any grape they got could be treated this way, attractively packaged in uniform portions. Delivered to customers' houses, by well-trained deliverymen who would also supply the other needed ingredients and could explain to buyers exactly what steps were required to "mature" the juice. "We could advertise," Jasper said. "Judiciously."

The dogs were barking again, and Henrietta tilted her head. "Emphasizing that everything ordered is legal," Jasper continued. Charlie, he explained, could help in the laboratory as they attempted to standardize the juice and the other products they'd package with it to form a home vintner's kit.

"You'd include some simple equipment," she suggested. "A thermometer, a hydrometer, premeasured yeast?"

"Something like that," Leo said. He made a note on a bit of paper and folded it carefully into his pocket. "If it went well, we might even try a champagne, or a sparkling burgundy."

"What does Didier think?" she asked.

"We haven't talked to him about it yet," he said. "It's not quite what he had in mind. But certainly it would help our case if Charlie was interested."

Dear Charlie, she thought. Of course he'd do it, if they asked. A way to help his family, and by extension to help some of the growers and drivers in town. He'd never leave, if he did that. Which meant Alice would never leave either, any more than she had herself. Charlie would do well at whatever he chose, but he had seemed so clearly meant for something else. If he went to her friend in Philadelphia, he might learn how to thread together a dinosaur's vertebrae, how to excavate a skull broken into a hundred bits. He might travel to China, to Siberia, to South America or the Arctic; he might live in New York.

She had such faith in him that when she received another letter from Philadelphia a few months later, she still refused to question her assessment of Charlie's gifts. *I'm disappointed, of course, to hear that your young friend has chosen another path instead of joining us*, Benjamin wrote. *But since I never received further word from him, it seems clear that not only is he not as interested as you implied, but that he is in some way deceiving you. I have no interest in admitting such a person to our program, although I do wish him—and you, always—the best of luck.* It was signed not "Benjamin" but "Benjamin N. Hardiman."

She would file that single sheet away, unable to piece the puzzle together—but on the night of the open house, she was still imagining, as she weighed Jasper and Leo's plans, that Benjamin had gotten Charlie's letters. Still imagining, as their conversation was suddenly interrupted by what had caught the dogs' interest, what Charlie might do in Pennsylvania.

A small red fox with a beautiful tail was running along the face of the cliff just above the dogs, a bit higher than they could reach when they stood on their hind legs, higher even than they could jump— darting from crevice to knob to bit of fern, sometimes slipping on a patch of ice and then leaping just beyond Olive's eager mouth and Oscar's paws to the next ledge. So little, so light, he seemed to float as he tried to reach the narrow ravine about fifty yards along the path, where the spring trickled down. The ravine, Henrietta could see, was too steep for the dogs to follow but would be easy enough for the fox to climb. Each time the fox neared the ravine, the dogs chased him away and sent him back across the cliff face in the opposite direction. Back, forth; north toward the lake, south toward the winery, as if he were writing a line of music with his paws. One shadow followed him on the lake side of the gazebo; two shadows on the winery side, where the lantern shone. Back and forth ran the fox, pursued by the dogs, now barking so persistently that Henrietta, looking back toward the house, could see faces at the windows. One belonged to Didier, who with a few remaining guests was sipping at the brandy that Jasper had wanted to offer Leo and Henrietta.

What were they doing out there, with the barking dogs? Jasper, Henrietta, Jasper's friend—whatever it was wouldn't matter, Didier thought. He would do what he could to save the family business, but he'd take care of his son no matter what happened. The letters Charlie had written to that professor would never be answered: because they had never been sent. Didier had seen the first one in the outgoing mail tray, and at the idea of his son following in his path, setting off for the same area at almost the same age, when anything could happen—he'd taken the letter and destroyed it.

He took the second one, too, and would have taken a third; he'd take as many as Charlie wrote. *Edward will let me go*, Chloe had said to him all those years ago, *but only if I leave Lawrence.* But in fact her bargain had been subtly, radically different. Last year, on the night after the amendment was ratified, they'd argued bitterly over whether they should bring Charlie into a business now on the verge of ruin. She destroyed a hatbox—a pretty one, too—crushing the cardboard bit by bit until nothing was left but a disk, and as the taupe stripes crumbled she let slip that Edward hadn't demanded Lawrence, not at first; he'd resisted, refused to let her take Charlie with her, and given in only when she offered Lawrence. She'd offered her first son—*So we could keep Charlie*, she said. *That's how far I'd go for him*—as a bribe. Since then he'd made some decisions without consulting her.

As he turned to say something to his boy, to offer him a taste from the special bottle, Charlie ran past him. Across the garden, over the snow, in his dress shoes and without his coat, he bounded toward Henrietta. She couldn't help it, her heart leapt toward him. He ran right past her, toward the rocks. The fox was tiring, the dogs were panting.

"Olive!" he shouted. "Oscar!"

To Henrietta's amazement, the dogs stopped and turned their hairy, intelligent faces his way. Her way. She had never had a dog.

"Come!" Charlie called. In that instant the fox found the ravine and sprinted up the shallow crease.

II

NATURAL HISTORY

AND THERE SHE WAS, WHEN I OPENED THE DOOR: DEIR-
dre, my old friend. She'd seen the cabin, which I'd bought back
when visitors to Silver Lake would have been hard pressed to guess
which of us would be better known. Some might have bet on me:
Rose Marburg. I published my papers and won my prizes early. The
wiser would have chosen Deirdre Banks.

On that August day in 2018, I opened the door after thirty years
and she said, stepping over the threshold and bumping into the
clumsy shelves, "I can't believe it's still the same."

"Pretty much," I said.

She eyed the old woodstove, the table and chairs, the slumping
couch. "Not exactly, but—you added a porch?"

"A few years ago."

She moved toward the screened-in space and sat where I'd hoped
she would, in the chair facing the kingbirds' nest. The male obligingly flicked down, scooped up a bee, and returned to his mate. I'd
tacked the porch onto the back of the cabin, which otherwise was
one high-peaked room centered around the chimney, with a sleeping loft over the front third, bathroom and cooking space tucked
beneath that. Once I'd imagined Deirdre visiting every year.

I left her watching the birds while I boiled water and found hibis-
cus tea for the pretty glass teapot she'd brought as a gift. Her hair

had changed since the treatments, but a clever stylist had shaped the coarse strands into chic feathery points. Long creases in front of her ears, deep folds in the skin of her neck, hands as veiny and spotted and dry as my own, with the cracked yellowish nails that came from years of working with chemicals in the lab. When we were young, she would have scheduled a manicure before the Silver Lake Gathering.

Two weeks every summer; a hundred or so structural biochemists; each time a different topic but always amazing talks, wild arguments, unexpected collaborations springing up among researchers sprawled on the large flat rock beside the lake or playing badminton poorly. We'd been invited first as postdocs, when the chance to go there meant everything; we primped before that first nervous arrival, and even after several summers we still painted our toenails and bought new shorts. I'd bought this cabin, which was four miles from the main gate of Silver Lake, after one of our visits. An easy drive even at night: and then, I'd crowed to Deirdre, no more sleeping in the infamous dormitories or sharing squalid bathrooms. I'd sleep in the loft and she could sleep on the couch near the woodstove whenever she wanted. We'd use it every summer.

Instead I'd dropped out of science and for years had hardly visited what was once my favorite part of the world. Sometimes I'd been able to rent the cabin out for the summer, which paid the taxes. Other years it sat empty save for the odd week or two, colonized by the mice who, when I returned, were reluctant to leave. Deirdre, who'd followed me into the kitchen, found one of them as she rummaged around for some sugar.

"The *fuck*?" she said, jumping back from the open cabinet.

Gently, apologizing, I nudged her aside and closed the door.

The creature, who had drowned in an inch of olive oil at the bottom of an old bottle lacking its cap, now floated belly-up, preserved like mouse confit. Pink paws, closed eyes. (Deirdre must have seen the paws.) I'd found it last fall, when I moved in full-time, and sometimes I imagined it talking to me. It, the other mice in the crawl space, the turkeys pterodactyling through the woods. The coyotes, who sang around the cabin at night. Sometimes it was so quiet that my own breath startled me.

To Deirdre, as if we were both city people and this was a rural joke, I said, "Isn't that odd? I found it before Christmas and it was so astonishing I hung on to it."

Deirdre knew a great deal about me, including the obvious facts: That, for a while, we'd worked in the same field of science, almost but not quite (we'd chosen different techniques to study the same problem) competing with each other. That just when I was becoming famous I left my lab to return to the village in central New York where I'd grown up, and where I taught high school for twenty-five years. I also wrote brief biographies, many for young readers, of women scientists: Dorothy Hodgkin, Rosalind Franklin. Barbara McClintock, Lucy Say. Later, when that sort of work grew more fashionable, I began writing magazine articles and then longer works for adults interested in science. I'd had a small success (the illustrations were lovely) with an overview of nineteenth-century women naturalists who, like Julia Ballard, specialized in moths and butterflies.

Deirdre knew all of this and more, but, as I reminded myself while she washed her hands, she'd still missed a lot. As I'd missed crucial things about her. She left the kitchen without touching anything, every surface apparently contaminated by the bottled mouse, and I poured the water and let the leaves and flowers steep. Then I brought the pot, along with the sugar Deirdre had forgotten about, back to the porch, where the tea glowed like rubies in the afternoon light. As I poured, she said, "I'm sorry about the school closing down."

"I was going to retire anyway," I said, adding, when she looked skeptical, "Really. I might have waited a few more years, but it was time, and I've saved some money. I'll be fine. It's terrible for the younger teachers, though. And for the village."

"All those students," she said. "Where will they go? If you and your sister were young now . . ."

"We would have been lost," I agreed. We talked for a minute about centralized school districts and school taxes, nothing very interesting, and then I asked about her work, and about her travels, and, cautiously, about her health. She was better, she claimed. Much better; and it seemed as though after all she'd have some years. Later we went for a walk, winding along the thin paths I'd traced through woods that were not legally mine but were close to abandoned. A little fox made his way up a cliff when he saw us, bits of shale falling as he leapt from layer to layer. A quail shot into the air. At the edge of a neighbor's pond, a young heron stabbed at a frog and missed, as if he didn't yet understand how the surface bent the light and made everything shift position. Deirdre, brushing at a cinnamon fern, said, "Would you come on Wednesday night? Sayeed wants me to talk about the early days of ubiquitin, since that's the topic this summer—"

"The new director?" I asked.

"Not so new," Deirdre said. "It's his sixth year. He chose Miriam's field for this summer, to help celebrate her seventy-fifth birthday."

Miriam Duskiewitz, who'd started as director when Deirdre and I were young, had been the first to welcome us to Silver Lake. "Some of the younger women," Deirdre continued, "thought that if I was going to give the opening address, it would be fun if I also talked a little about what it was like in the old days, when Miriam first took over, and how much she changed things. I said I would—which is why you should come. You're as much a part of that time as I am."

"You know I don't go there," I said. She was walking behind me and couldn't see my face. "Even if I'm around, I head out of town during the Gathering. I stayed to meet you, because you asked, but—"

"But this is different," she said. Adding not, as I dreaded: *Because I've been sick. Because I don't know how many times we'll get to see each other again*, but, "Because you'd be keeping me company, coming as my friend. And lots of people you used to know will be around, to celebrate Miriam—it's a good way for you to reconnect. And Miriam would like it."

"Miriam," I said. I hadn't seen her in so long.

"And," Deirdre said helpfully, "you could meet some of the younger crowd, maybe find some subjects for your articles about contemporary women scientists."

WE'D BEEN THE younger crowd when we first went to Silver Lake, both of us in our early twenties. And after I cooked us dinner and we returned to the porch—candles now, and a kerosene lamp; Irish whiskey rather than tea; coyotes howling—Deirdre and I got to talking about the summer we met, in a very different place: the research institute where I'd done my postdoc, in a suburb north of Philadelphia. There'd been a party at my advisor's house, a great stew of people, a panic caused when my sister, Bianca, had taken an elderly visiting scientist on a little jaunt and failed to return him until very late. After that party I could never pretend that Bianca and I, who'd once been so close, weren't on utterly different paths. Deirdre, just starting her postdoc at Penn, had been there as well.

The day had been so chaotic that I barely registered meeting the young woman she was then. Deirdre remembered events more clearly. On the porch, watching bats suck insects from the sky, I said, "Who brought you there? You can't have just shown up."

"Dr. Athyn," she said. "My advisor at Penn. You didn't really know him. And then there were two guys from his lab that *I* hardly knew. I'd only moved there a couple of weeks earlier."

She hadn't wanted to go to the party at all, especially not with them, but Dr. Athyn, who went every year, insisted. A farewell celebration for the visiting scientists who'd spent their summer at the fancy research institute twenty minutes from their own lab: Who would miss *that*?

Into his Chevy Nova she'd gone, sitting behind Lev, the research associate who'd set up her equipment, and next to Jiazhen, her fellow postdoc. Dr. Athyn drove too fast through the steaming Philadelphia streets and then into outskirts that were leafier but not cooler, shouting facts from a new paper she hadn't read. Still talking, he parked down the street from a tall hedge with a rank smell and then popped them through the gate. Around the bland façade of the house, past the azaleas and tired begonias (I knew those azaleas well, but by then had stopped noticing them): and there was the pool, and the cloth-draped table, the paired grills, the disordered lawn chairs separating various groups. Lev and Jiazhen peeled away but Dr. Athyn taxonomized the crowd for Deirdre: Indian biochemists here, Argentinian structural biologists there. Japanese crystallographers, Finnish membrane biologists, French enzymologists by the zebra grass. Farther away, near the pergola and the fountain—

"But there," Deirdre said, interrupting herself, "was Constance."

She was talking about my advisor: Constance Humboldt, no longer living, but on that day unabashedly scratching her bosom while listening intently to a good-looking young man.

"How intimidated was I?" Deirdre said.

All the scientists sprouting from the smooth green lawn were Constance's colleagues and students: I knew them by then, I took them for granted. And Dr. Athyn claimed Constance as *his* old friend, as well as his greatest rival, someone Deirdre would have to reckon with if she stayed in this field. Tall, heavy, with a low-cut caftan stretched over her large chest and larger waist before stopping abruptly above her shapely knees and calves, she'd looked to Deirdre like Gertrude Stein but for the long hair wound in a knot and stabbed with two lacquered sticks.

Caught in Constance's orbit, surrounded by Constance's clever friends, Deirdre, she said, had felt entirely average. (Never, I thought. Never.) Averagely tall, averagely built, with unremarkable dirty blond hair above hazel eyes and heavy eyebrows; in a photo she would, she'd thought (but she'd be wrong about this: the eyebrows were gone and she was now quite slight but still utterly recognizable), be the one who, twenty years later, no one could name. She'd done excellent but not brilliant work in graduate school, where her thesis supervisor had ignored her flair for seeing unexpected patterns and had written such bland recommendations that she'd ended up at her third-choice lab for her postdoctoral fellowship.

That day, she said, she was still wondering if this would work out. The university was fine but the neighborhood around it was seedier than she'd expected. The lab itself was overcrowded and she'd been discouraged to find that most of the postdocs and grad students were men, while all but one of the technicians were women. Whether this reflected Dr. Athyn's attitudes, Lev's, or both, she couldn't yet tell. Also the project that Dr. Athyn had suggested for her had more to do with fitting into the framework of his big NIH grant than with her own interests.

But she wouldn't, she'd told herself, be the one fetching the beef livers from the slaughterhouse. Or the one refining the protocols for preparing the liver homogenate, or isolating and purifying the enzyme, or cleaning up afterwards; there were advantages to joining such a large and well-funded lab, even if those luxuries— who was she, not to be washing her own cuvettes?—increased the pressure. She had no excuse not to do dazzling work: an insight so terrifying that, sweating lightly in the late-afternoon sun, abandoned by her new colleagues, she stepped back a few paces, thinking she might disappear for a while, and knocked a drink from the hand of a camel-faced man so tall that she found herself apologizing to his neck.

"Roger!" I said, still following her story intently.

"Of course," she said. Roger Bakmanian, who dabbed piña colada from his shirt as he reassured Deirdre, chatting amiably until she relaxed enough for him to reveal that he was married to Constance. His eyelashes were wonderfully long and he played contrabassoon in the city orchestra. Learning that Deirdre played the oboe, he immediately pulled her over to his wife. Perhaps because it was Roger rather than Dr. Athyn who presented her, and because he emphasized not her status as a new postdoc at Penn but her gifts as a double reed player, Constance seemed to warm to her right away. Later Deirdre would understand, as I'd learned before her, that the surest way to Constance's heart was to be kind to her somewhat undervalued husband. Within minutes Constance had invited her to come up Sunday afternoon and play with Roger and his friends.

And then, Deirdre recollected, the croquet game being played near the magnolia tree had grown boisterous as Constance talked about the Berg *Kammerkonzert*, which Roger's group, until now lacking an oboe, longed to tackle, and then about the merits of the city orchestra, her own work, her bathroom renovations, and the reshufflings taking place at the institute. Deirdre had nodded, murmured, and tried to make intelligent comments. Tried not to mind that Dr. Athyn, when he strolled past, rolled his eyes as if he thought Deirdre had engineered exactly this conversation.

"And remember the pool?" Deirdre said.

Still I saw that large tiled swimming pool, below the edge of the terrace and away from the croquet game, in my dreams. That day it had been surrounded by people. As the afternoon wore on, Deirdre either met or had pointed out to her Rick and Wen-li, Diego and Vivek. She talked briefly with Utpal, who was from Bangalore, and with Stanislaw, who came from Warsaw. She met Jocelyn, Anisha, and Winifred, and also two older men named Arnold and Herb, although she couldn't remember which had won the Nobel Prize. She spoke briefly to Edmund, Jamaican but educated in England, and to Keshia, who'd been raised in Brooklyn. The sun burned above the water and the chickens burned on the grill. For a while, she held a platter for an amiable man with wisps of white car hair while he tonged chicken onto the glossy surface. Fu'ad cannonballed into the pool, sending up a column of spray that rained down on her arms. Croquet was abandoned for badminton, badminton for drinks; the sky dimmed and a long low beam picked out a fountain with a fluted rim, to the side of the yard, into which fat bubbles emerging from a piece of hollow bamboo periodically fell. (My sister had caused those bubbles, but I wouldn't learn that for years and had never told Deirdre.)

"And there was another pool," Deirdre said. "At the very back of the yard. More of a pond, really. Remember that?"

I did, but not with the same intensity. Wanting a few minutes' escape from the flurry of names and faces, Deirdre had walked down the gentle slope to that rough pool generated by some invisible spring. Grass grew right to the edge, drooping tips brushing the surface, and she leaned over to watch the tadpoles startled by her shadow. A voice off to her right said, "Don't fall in," which almost made her do just that. Two men about her age sat on a rough wooden bench beneath the willow, smiling from behind the long branches either at her or—

"At *you*," she said. "That's when I first saw you, when you called out to me. You were wearing your hair very short then. You walked over to me and touched my arm and said, '*You're* new.'"

That moment I did remember, although many of the other details she reported were missing from my own memory. Half my mind, most of my mind, had been wondering all evening what my sister was up to.

"Visiting?" she said I'd said.

She'd replied that she was and introduced herself, adding, "Dr. Athyn brought me, from the university. I just started in his lab."

I was embarrassed to remember so little of this. Not that Deirdre had been less important to me than I was to her; far from it. Just that at that party, as would be true for so much of my life in science and more recently too, I was looking in the wrong direction.

I had, she continued, told her that I was finishing up my second year with Constance, and then offered to introduce her to my friends on the bench—which was when she'd first met Ehud Yarden and Itzhak Sonnenberg, who would shape her entire professional life. That day, she said, she missed their last names and also confused who was the primary investigator and who his slightly younger postdoc, but she did grasp that they'd been visiting for eight weeks, working in the lab of one of Constance's colleagues, and were about to head home. And that they'd slipped away from this party with two bottles of wine—"And with *you*," she said, "don't you remember?"—and were now telling stories about Herb and tossing twigs at the pond.

"I thought you were involved with one of them," Deirdre said, which made us both laugh. Ehud, she continued, had passed her a bottle, and after taking a swig she'd replied to his question about what she was working on without revealing any details, a caution she'd already learned. Fluorescence studies of the steady-state kinetics of ordered-sequential NAD-dependent enzyme systems, she'd said. Or something like that.

Itzhak asked if it was a ternary system and she'd nodded and swigged more of the cool white wine. Then, as a burst of music swept over the yard and was quickly damped, she asked the reciprocal question and I, who'd been loaned to the pair for much of that summer by Constance, answered enthusiastically for all of us.

"You did," she said, when I protested. "I'm sure you did."

Although by then, she admitted now, she might not have been paying full attention. The sun cast long rays over the water, highlighting the fringe of grass and the leaves on the willow branches. A small fish splashed. Dragonflies chased by swallows needled the air. They were messing around, Deirdre said I'd said, with a small protein discovered just a few years earlier but since identified in all sorts of eukaryotic cells: hence its name, ubiquitin. What did it do? (That's how long ago this was: 1979, we truly didn't know anything.) Somehow, Itzhak said, it played a role in cellular protein degradation. But it's not clear, Ehud said, how that might work. Not clear at all.

I tried to imagine what Deirdre had felt like then, before I really knew her, before our work lives had grown so intertwined. Before any of that work was interesting to anyone but us. Once, at a dinner party in Boston, I'd explained my work to a stranger in the simplest possible terms: ubiquitin molecules, I'd told him, bind to other proteins and mark them for degradation. Without that marking and breaking down, nothing in the cell can work; the cell needs the parts of the old dead proteins to make new proteins. Life from death. The look on his face, half puzzlement and half boredom, helped me later, when I was writing my first sketches of women in science.

Sitting around that seeping pond, Deirdre said, she drank more than she intended. While the sun sank lower and the swallows sped along the surface of the water, she heard something about the odd conundrum that protein degradation requires energy, when it ought not to; something about the sequence of the amino acids in the small protein. Also, Deirdre claimed, I told a story about my sister and a sailboat she'd capsized in a distant lake. The next morning she woke with a headache and a sense that she'd missed some crucial things.

SHE WOULDN'T SLEEP at the cabin; despite all we'd had to drink, she insisted on driving to Silver Lake and settling into the tidy square house where they put the most honored guests. The following evening—she'd talked me into this—I drove into the parking lot well before her talk was due to start. I knew where to go, still; the buildings, once part of a boys' camp, had been fringed with ramps and freshly painted, but mostly the place looked the same and there was something reassuring about watching the stragglers, too late for dinner, hauling suitcases from their cars and bumping them over the gravel as they made their baffled way toward the identical dorms. Acres of roughly mown grass dotted with buildings large and small, oriented not to each other but to a stand of trees or a garden or the wavering paths connecting them. To the south, inconveniently far from the parking lot, stretched the curved row of long, narrow dormitories, two stories high, the shingled sides painted white and green and pierced by windows that rattled in the slightest breeze. A wide porch fronted each, unlit but for one small bulb over each door, ensuring that the names carved there—*Colden, Haystack, Wolfjaw, Gothics*; the buildings were named after Adirondack peaks—were nearly impossible to read.

That we walked into the wrong buildings, into the wrong rooms, might have been intentional; when I thought about the place, as I did so often after I stopped going there, I wondered if those confusions had been designed to throw us off-balance. In the cabin, through all the past months, feeling the pull of Silver

Lake across the four miles of rough woods and dirt roads, willing myself not to drive there, not to walk down the paths or peer in the windows of buildings shut for the season, I had many times reconstructed the setting in my mind. Tried to remember my first views of it; then tried to remember the middle years, my fourth, fifth, sixth visits, when it felt more like home than any place I'd ever known and when I believed myself to be a permanent part of it. Then, so happy I could be generous, I'd helped the newcomers, remembering how nothing would feel easy or comfortable at first and how even getting there, to this spot between the High Peaks and Lake Champlain, would have been hard for them. Newcomers would fly into Burlington and take the ferry across the lake, then get lost trying to make their way along the back roads; or they'd fly into Albany and drive hours north and get lost; or they'd take the train to Westport without realizing there wouldn't be any cabs. In their rooms they'd find spiders, chipmunks, bats, beetles, mold in the showers, sometimes toads; inside and outside intermingled, and we froze when it rained, baked when it was hot. No one minded, once they'd settled in. We danced in the same room where we gave our talks and swam in the freezing pond (which was all it was, not a lake after all) after which the place had been named, and in a meadow across the narrow road we drank while watching the Perseids shower down.

I went toward the lecture hall. I was wearing my glasses; my once short black hair was now chin-length and gray; I was thirty years older and no one recognized me. Deirdre was waiting for me just outside the double doors, which still hung crookedly on their hinges but were diminished by an outdoor bulb's harsh glare. Some safety-minded person (not Miriam, I thought; she used to love the velvety dark) had installed these all over, casting on the paths and porches a disturbing blue light. We chatted for a bit while the seats filled up, and then I claimed a spot in the front, at the end of the row. Deirdre went up to the podium and straightened her scarf.

In the years since we'd stopped working together I'd seen her give talks and seminars, several times at Cornell and twice in Boston, but those had been purely science, updates on the work of her lab that I attended not to keep up—my field had exploded, I couldn't have followed all that was happening even if I'd wanted to—but because she was my friend, and always busy, and this was a way we could be together. I'd never seen her do this sort of thing before, though, an overview and appreciation to a large room of mingled strangers and friends, and I had no idea how polished she'd grown.

She spoke, first, about Silver Lake as an institution: how miraculous it was that each summer it rose, Brigadoon-like, from this space between the lake and the mountains, filling with structural biochemists from near and far who would share ideas from fields that to outsiders looked nearly identical but were, to us, as different as knitting and baseball. What we had in common were the molecules of life, but we drew from different areas of physics, biology, and chemistry, studied different aspects of different molecules, different reactions in different contexts using wildly different techniques. It was amazing, in a way, that we could talk to each other at all: yet each year we did, always to surprising benefit. Even within her own field, Deirdre said, the simple problems she'd confronted as a very young scientist—What *was* ubiquitin? What did it do? How did it do it?—had like everything split into scores of smaller fields as the true complexity revealed itself.

Briefly, charmingly, she sketched out the major leaps, work her collaborators Ehud and Itzhak had done that would later result in a Nobel Prize. She left out her own groundbreaking work and the furor around her omission from that prize, but instead (thoughtful friend) she smiled in my direction and mentioned a paper I'd published in the mid-1980s, which had made a little splash. After leaping through the huge advances that had followed the discovery of the different roles played by polyubiquitin signals, she then sketched even more briefly the trajectories for other crucial areas represented by those in the audience. Each summer, she said, the director's choice of a central topic forced us all to think more broadly, move away from our narrow specializations, open ourselves to new ideas and techniques—and with this, she led us to the evening's real purpose. The topic Sayeed had announced last fall—the nature of the protein degradation system—was a beautiful way to bring us all together while celebrating both the institution of Silver Lake and the vital role played by Miriam during her years as director.

Everyone clapped and Sayeed, sitting in the front row just to Deirdre's left, bowed his head modestly. After Deirdre applauded him she shifted her gaze to the center of the room, where Miriam sat in a striped linen dress and the earrings (I remembered those earrings) she had always worn on opening nights.

"When I first came here in the early 1980s," Deirdre said, speaking directly to Miriam, "at the very beginning of my career, there were hardly any women. Just a handful of us, each invited by Miriam. We found each other right away, we stuck together, we made friends. Much of what we've done since wouldn't have happened without her example and her support."

The applause lasted a long time, continuing until everyone rose and Miriam, blushing furiously, stood herself and bowed. When she sat, a tall woman in a peach dress stood up near the back of the hall and spoke for a minute about her first visit here, in 1986: Wilma Gregten, I remembered her. Then Rebecca Yagoda stood up, three rows below Wilma, and spoke about her first visit in 1987, when she'd met Wilma. Rachel Pruett spoke next, about the work she, Rebecca, and Wilma had done together after meeting here; then a younger woman I didn't know stood up near the front to talk about visiting in the mid-nineties, after studying in Rachel's lab. An Indian woman in a green skirt spoke, then a woman with a Belgian accent, then a woman who said that the ideas she brought from Silver Lake to her lab in Venezuela had spread through a whole generation of graduate students. Eleven women altogether, each connected to one or more of the others and all invited by Miriam; the twelfth was Deirdre, who'd welcomed Wilma (I had too; we'd disposed of the petrified mouse she found in her pillow) all those years ago.

This, Deirdre said when they were done, was what Miriam had given them. Given us, she said, looking again in my direction. Whatever she said after that, outlining the next days' program, was compact and gracious and promptly forgotten.

I TRIED TO slip away when the crowd tumbled out, but Deirdre caught me by the arm and insisted I come to the reception in the lounge where, when we were young, we'd spent so many hours. "I wanted you to see all those women," she said. "To remember what it was like when it was still fun. Wasn't it fun, then?"

"It was," I said. Once she would have caught everything folded into those words, but these days I was able to conceal from her the knotted feelings that even my solitary walks in the woods couldn't untangle. "Thank you for reminding me."

I had loved my work for a while, loved sharing it with Deirdre and others—and then I didn't. My father died, my sister disappeared, some other things happened and all I could see was what a business science had become. Money (there was never enough, not even in the biggest labs), politics, grant-writing, speech-making; all of us struggling for recognition, envying and competing with each other while the actual work we'd trained to do contracted to a slim bright thread. The wonder, gone. The looking and thinking and experimenting, the quest to make sense of the world as we found it: all that, gone.

I began to say I don't know what but stopped when I saw Deirdre's face in the light of an open door. Very happy; totally exhausted. Unlike me, she'd been able to keep hold of the bright thread. I kept my mouth shut long enough to be spared by the roar inside the lounge, which was already full when we got there.

Arms reached eagerly for Deirdre, pulling her toward the fireplace and the group around Miriam, and as I stepped back and took a glass of red wine from the tray of one of the uniformed young people moving among us (we used to bring our own cheap beer), a wonderfully freckled woman introduced herself to me. A biochemical entomologist, she said, studying the degradation of muscle proteins during holometabolous metamorphosis: ubiquitin-mediated, of course. Was I speaking later in the week?

"Just visiting," I said, delighted to have found in this dangerous room a person I didn't know from my past. "I'm an old friend of Deirdre's."

"I thought so, from the way she looked at you during her talk. Then you're a ubiquitin person too?"

I gave her the short version, the party version, of how I'd left science to become a high school teacher and ended up writing biographies of women scientists. Most people would have moved away then, after a polite comment, but she asked who I'd written about and, after I'd mentioned the most obvious names, who I was studying now.

"A woman you wouldn't know," I said. "Someone who taught natural history to children for a long time. She was born before the Civil War and lived through Prohibition times."

"And you found her—how?" A group of freckles on one cheek drew together as she smiled.

"We're related," I said. No point trying to explain our complicated family tree. Some people, not many, remember my grandmother Alice and her sisters Agnes, Marion, Caroline, and Elaine, who'd helped raise me and my sister. No one remembers *their* aunt: Henrietta Atkins. In the building where I went to school—the same place where Henrietta had taught, and where, later, I'd return to teach: now shuttered, now shut, all those histories trapped inside—I used to dream about what my life would be when I escaped from the place I then despised. I thought my teachers were stupid. My classmates baffled me. Our little village and the surrounding farms offered nothing I could imagine anyone wanting. From the classroom windows on the school's west side I could see the lakeshore road on which, when I was eleven, my mother had been killed by a speeding car.

Before her death my mother had told me some stories about Henrietta; later my grandfather Leo, who'd known Henrietta when she was old and he was young, told me more. He'd shown me photos of her: standing, at the 1911 high school graduation, in front of her eldest niece, Marion Cummings. With her youngest niece, my grandmother Alice; with the student who became my other grandfather, Charles. Long gone, all of them, along with the docks and warehouses and flying fields and factories, the dirigibles moored in the narrow ravine. The steamboats gone, the airplanes gone. Then Leo gone as well, followed by our old house and the winery, which my father sold before he died, and Henrietta's house, turned into a bed-and-breakfast. The high school was still there, though, and when I started teaching, standing in classrooms where Henrietta herself had stood while diagramming a bat or a bee, I had sometimes felt myself dissolving in a way that delighted me. Me, my sister, my mother; her mother and father and their parents; my mother's aunts and *their* aunt; the friends and neighbors and lovers and enemies of all those people, over so many years. Little molecules combining, as needed, into something larger, separating again when the tasks were complete.

The freckled woman—Nelly, she'd announced—regarded me curiously; I'd been silent too long. "A lot of those women naturalists are really interesting," she said. "Not just the work they did, but how they did it."

"I think so too," I said, warming to her. All around us people gathered, swerved, split into streams like starlings. Nelly's gaze shifted over my shoulder.

"I'm sure my aunt would be fascinated," she said. "You know how curious she is about our predecessors."

One of Silver Lake's fabled charms, as I'd learned during my first visits, was the uncanny frequency of coincidences. Not just overlaps of interests and knowledge, but moments when two apparent strangers discovered they'd been in the same kindergarten class, or traveled through Greenland a month apart, or slept with the same person. Even so, as Miriam came around my shoulder and kissed Nelly on the cheek, this felt unreasonable.

"Rose," Miriam said, "I almost didn't recognize you! It's so good to see you."

I might have had the same trouble recognizing her, if she hadn't stood up at Deirdre's talk. Her voice was still the same, though, strong and warm and somehow caressing, even with those she barely knew. As a server extended between us a tray of flaky mushroom pastries, I managed a few phrases about how well Miriam looked, how glad I was to see her celebrated as she deserved. How pleasing Deirdre's talk had been, pulling together so many people from the past.

"Even you," she said. "After all this time."

"Even me," I agreed.

Miriam pursed her lips, lifted two pastries onto napkins, and handed one to Nelly. "I see you've met my niece."

They looked nothing alike, but when they bit into the little disks, they inclined their heads forward in just the same way, so that two parallel streams of flakes showered to the floor. Nelly crumpled up her napkin and said, "Rose is writing about one of her ancestors, a woman who studied and taught natural history a hundred years ago."

"Really?" Miriam said. Having trained us, when we were young, to describe our projects clearly, she finished her pastry and waited. *We don't get points for being vague*, she used to say. *You're doing something wrong if you can't explain your project to any intelligent person.* I'd written plenty about Henrietta by then and should have been able to say something clever: she wrote an excellent pamphlet about sphinx moths, some fossils she collected were still in the cabinets at Cornell. Instead I stood mute and awkward, living testament to the particular stupidity Henrietta and I shared.

"I read your book about the lady lepidopterists," Miriam continued, covering my silence. "*Butterfly Ladies*? *Butterfly Women*? *Ladies and Moths*? Sorry, I forget the title. I meant to write you about it."

"I don't think you did," I said faintly. Deirdre, still near the fireplace, was talking with great enthusiasm to a man I didn't recognize. The book—until that moment the one I'd been happiest to see in the stores—suddenly seemed ridiculous.

Miriam raised one twisted and swollen-knuckled hand to an earring. "I suppose writing about your relative is a natural next step. But if you're going to write about scientists, instead of *doing* science—why don't you write about us?"

"Us?"

She circled her forefinger through the air, gathering all the bodies, and then looked over toward Deirdre. "Or just write about the two of you, if the whole crowd seems like too much."

"There's Rowan," Nelly said, rescuing me. "We should go."

Obediently Miriam followed Nelly toward a group clustered by the sofas. The largest group, in fact, composed of the women who'd spoken after Deirdre. How close they stood! I couldn't remember doing that; always, I kept only one or two people near. I had to wait for Deirdre to see me and peel herself away before saying goodbye.

I thanked her, not as fully as I should have, for luring me out and giving me one more chance to visit this place. Her talk, I said, had been wonderful. "You struck just the right note," I said. "I could see how delighted Miriam was."

"It meant a lot to me that you were here," she said. "And I'm so glad you had a minute with Miriam. But wouldn't you like to stay for a while?" She scanned my face, waiting for some indication that I was glad to see the people we'd once found essential. Some assurance that our friendship would not continue to attenuate.

"Let's have lunch," I said. "Next week, before you leave."

"Meet me here?"

I shook my head. "Come to my place." She promised that she would.

Not until I got back to the cabin and collapsed on the porch did I start breathing normally.

SOMETIMES, WHEN YOU'VE been consumed by a scientific problem for a while, a fresh idea can rise up from what appears to be nothing and sweep through your head like a wave. It's winter, now: snow on the ground, tracks in the snow, coyote scat solid with rabbit skin near the tracks. Henrietta, as she had since I'd left our village and moved into the cabin full-time, accompanied me through the rest of the summer and the fall, although I said nothing about the project and hid my papers when Deirdre came by for lunch before leaving Silver Lake. As soon as she left I went back to work, seeing more clearly than before what might be hiding in my pages. Often

I don't know what I mean; when I try to say what I mean, I lie; it seems I only tell the truth when I'm talking about someone else. In those sketches of Henrietta's world, my own experiences had metamorphosed. Soon, I thought, when I finished writing about her, I might try something new, related to what Miriam had suggested. Something for Deirdre, a sketch of us at Silver Lake that was but also wasn't us. If I translated some events, deleted some and transposed others, changed the names but kept the feelings, kept *our* feelings . . . ?

A LONG TIME ago, a woman who believed she could cure almost anything with fresh air, a vegetable diet, nude sunbathing, and good conversation built a colony where her followers could gather. This was in the Adirondack Mountains, not far from Lake Champlain: the main building, which stood for almost a century, was big and white, with four floors in the central section. Long dormitories angled out on either side, with outbuildings behind those and then, further west but before the mountains began to rise, a small cold lake surrounded by pine and hemlock trees. In front were pillared porches, where guests could admire the view to the east. The shutters were green; also the doors and the trim; also the staircases leading from the central porch and the dormitories to the narrow lawn. After the lawn came the dirt road and then the fan-shaped hayfield, which as it widened sloped toward more woods. Beyond the trees lay a shallow river.

Later a golf course replaced the field and houses rose around the edges—but in 1988, you could stand on the steps and look out over those open acres, covered with high grass or, a bit later in the season, with hay cut and raked into windrows. A tractor turned the rows into small square bales, which flew up from the ground and into the wagon behind. Swallows followed the wagon. Crickets popped into the air. Somewhere there was a barn, which housed the hay.

The colony was still charming then, and families who'd come there for decades, and who didn't mind the mice, the splinters, the jammed doors and slanted floors, rented it out for reunions and weddings. Various groups and societies, quite different from those who'd once tried to recover their health there, also booked it for meetings and conferences—among them a small but influential gathering of structural biochemists who met there each August.

Because it was near the mountains, the summers were usually delightfully cool and the buildings weren't air-conditioned. A heat wave during the 1988 meeting made the afternoons stuffy, but the scientists coped by abandoning the meeting rooms and giving their presentations on the shaded porches or beneath the trees on the lawn. Sometimes a page from a lecture blew away, or an easel supporting a poster tipped over. The younger scientists found a kind of pleasure in this: their elders in shorts, with sweaty hair, chasing papers through the hydrangeas.

On the first afternoon of that year's meeting, two young women who'd been there before walked through the uncut field talking about their earliest visit, when they'd been slotted into tiny attic rooms in the oldest dormitory. Famously hot, famously airless. Usually assigned to the youngest and most obscure of the participants. Who'd be stuck there now? They talked about the year it had rained every day, the year the sugar maple was hit by lightning, the year Mihaly dropped dead on the tennis court. A sound they couldn't at first identify—someone playing a clarinet in the trees near the porch—joined the crickets' background buzz.

They followed the serpentine path, an S linking the central building and the trees across the field, back toward the sound. (The women, who didn't and wouldn't have children, thought not about the links between generations but between friends, and ideas.) Their view shifted every few yards. First they faced the front entrance squarely. Then the dormitories to the north; then the front again; the south-facing dorms and the front again. Whoever mowed the path had probably intended that effect, which made the women forget they weren't invisible. No one would walk through the thigh-high grass without the path, which even the breeze seemed to follow. No one would flush the turkeys from their hiding places, or surprise the snakes, or hear the blackbirds and finches and hawks and crows: so many calls and cries that the sound of the clarinet almost got lost.

As the women (Rosalind—always Rosalind, never Roz—and Dee) wondered aloud who would be on the porch, rows of white clouds overtook them. The bottom surfaces of the clouds were gray and the grass beneath their shadows turned lavender, olive, umber, and then green again. Rows of clouds rolled from west to east over the buildings and then over the lawn and the road and finally them. Rosalind pointed out a former lover. Dee, scanning the ninety-odd figures swarming up and around the stairs, found two former students. They'd know many more, of course, people who like them had attended this meeting for years. But there'd be new people too, awkward and nervous, jet-lagged if they'd flown in from France or California, perhaps missing their luggage or absurdly dressed: no one ever got that right the first time. Dee, brushing a grasshopper from her leg, realized that, in rushing directly from the research institute where she worked, she'd left her sneakers behind.

"Take mine," Rosalind said. In the six years they'd been coming here, they'd shared shirts, cigarettes, books, liquor, data, friends, and more; everything, really, except for their equally large but different gifts and their unequal social skills. During the long drive from her lab in Chicago, she'd pondered those differences, which were part of what drew her and Dee together and made them good collaborators. "I have an extra pair," she added.

Dee made a face and pointed at her feet, three sizes smaller than Rosalind's, and then they both laughed. A line of music looped around them as they climbed, still laughing, up the central stairs; a thick humming rose from the gathered humans struggling to be heard; from behind the hills (the clouds continued to roll from west to east, larger now, a few somewhat darker) came a rumbling that might have been distant thunder. Two of the more senior investigators—Marianne and Charlene, who'd first invited Rosalind and Dee when they were postdocs, and still watched over them—stepped out from behind the vines to greet them.

For a few minutes, just long enough for Rosalind and Dee to feel noticed and welcomed, they chatted; then the older women deftly handed them off to some younger men. (A skill, Rosalind had realized by then, and one at which both Marianne and Charlene excelled. She admired them intensely without wanting to emulate them; even Dee, with her excellent intuitions, was never sure what they really thought.) Protein chemists, NMR spectroscopists, specialists in enzymatic cascades or phosphorylation, old and young but most of them men, which didn't seem so odd then. Of the few women present, several (thank Dorothy Hodgkin: a single woman, as Marianne frequently noted, could make an amazing difference to a field) were crystallographers. Few knew much about ubiquitination. From the trees to the south, a sliver of darkness detached itself from the dark trunk of a white pine: a young woman, carrying that clarinet. "Sissa's daughter," someone murmured. They were not allowed to bring family or guests, but Sissa, a distant descendant of the original owner, managed the grounds.

Four chemists from Bordeaux who shared Dee's interests pounced on her before she reached the front door, and Rosalind, who that summer was as famous as she'd ever be, made her way into the lobby. She greeted a dark-haired toxicologist from Mississippi with a gap between his two front teeth. A plump Kashmiri peptide chemist with a wonderful laugh. A tiny German woman studying hindered phenols, in her eighties but so energetic she might have been twenty, ruffling her apricot-tinted hair, and beside her a very tall woman with the aspect of a heron. A stranger stood in front of her mailbox: tall, wearing bicycle shorts and a T-shirt, his long blond hair pulled back in a ponytail.

"Could you?" she asked, gesturing.

"Sorry," he said, stepping aside. His name, he offered, was Sebastian Kent. Something—bicycle grease?—dotted the tanned skin beneath the burnished hairs of one forearm. She opened the mailbox and took out the schedule of talks for the first two days, a notice about a cocktail party, and a postcard, identical to the one she'd received last August, from the man in Chicago she'd been seeing for several years but wasn't serious about. (That's how long ago this was: no Web, no email, no cell phones. Veterans brought rolls of change for the telephone booths.)

"Could you," Sebastian echoed as she turned, "show me how to work this?"

She'd met Dee in just this way; during their first visit, their mailboxes, like their airless rooms, had been adjacent. Each box bore two rickety dials, meant to be spun to etched letters and numbers now so worn they were almost unreadable. Someone had shown Dee, who in turn had shown Rosalind, the trick of guessing the right positions and releasing the latch. Now Rosalind passed this on to Sebastian, who bent close to her face as he followed her movements.

"Pretty shirt," he said as he straightened up, gesturing toward the garment she'd carefully chosen to look careless.

"It's old," she said (it had been her sister's: but she'd lost her sister, a story no one knew but Dee). Surprised by the flush rising warmly up her neck, she turned to hide her confusion before adding (where *was* Dee?), "You should check your box a few times a day—it's how the organizers find us."

A fat bumblebee carried into the lobby a shard of the human buzz that continued to rise on the porch. Then the crowd followed the bumblebee, into the lobby and out the back door, all headed toward the large meeting room and the first of many talks. Dee found Rosalind in time for them to sit together.

BY THE TIME the talk was over, the sky had darkened and a wind had risen; in the dining hall, Rosalind could hardly hear Dee for the clatter of silverware and the clamor of voices, the rattle of windows in the wind, the harsh croaks of the crows settling hurriedly into their roosts. While they ate rice and fish and greens, the thunderstorm sent thick sheets of water down the walls and windows, rain so violent that the sky turned black and they had to turn on the lights, yet so brief that by the time they were drinking coffee, the late-evening sun was once more beaming through the windows and making the roof-drips glitter. Rosalind went out onto the porch with Dee, inhaling the sharp air as she once would have inhaled the smoke from a cigarette. A heavyset man from Israel with white wisps of ear hair came up and peeled Dee away, leaving Rosalind alone to watch the flitting damselflies. Surely those black-winged ones, with their iridescent emerald bodies, had not been here in previous years?

"Ebony jewelwings," said Sebastian, materializing beside her. "Those are always fun. My brother used to study dragonflies and damselflies. You know" (she did not know), "the odonatids. But"—he grasped her shoulders lightly and spun her, as if they were waltzing, toward the right—"look over here. Isn't that odd?"

He pointed toward the tall pines off to the side of the porch, where Sissa's daughter and her clarinet had earlier detached herself from the tree. White foam was streaming down the craggy bark of the trunks, splitting and re-forming around the stubs and then gathering into frothy petticoats at the roots.

"What *is* that?" Rosalind said. "Are they sick?" The foam seemed to be jetting from the cracks.

"They're fine," Sebastian said. "It's just chemistry—it's been so hot and so dry, for so long, that the trunks got coated with all sorts of salt and acid particles from the air. When the water hits those, it makes a kind of soap. Then it foams as it runs over the bark."

How had she not learned that before? Later that week, when they were deep in a fling Rosalind believed she'd concealed from everyone but Dee (and even Dee didn't know about Sebastian's lost brother), the number of coincidences required to bring about that moment made them laugh. Why, on the night of their first meeting, should there have been a heavy rain at just that place and time, falling after such hot, dry weather, producing the phenomenon Rosalind hadn't noticed before but which Sebastian (initially trained as a plant physiologist; now screening fungi used by folk healers and determining the structures of the active antimicrobial compounds) was exactly the right person to explain? And why did he get to explain it to someone who'd care?

In public she tried to ignore him, having learned on her first visit that nothing diminished a woman in this place as fast as an attachment to one of the men. She avoided him at breakfast, at the morning poster sessions, at the afternoon and evening talks. At dinner she listened to him discussing the mountains of data gathered by Darwin—pigeons! Had anyone ever written so much about pigeons?—as if he were just another acquaintance passing along a familiar tale. Between the talks, she floated around before settling

down next to Dee, scribbling notes while speakers defined the structure of retroviral proteases. There were groups from Paris and groups
from Poland; talks attended only by specialists in that area and talks
for which, despite the heat, they all crowded into the largest meeting
room. Rosalind's talk, about polyubiquitin chains, was one of those.

The success of her presentation was, she mistakenly thought,
the most important part of her visit that year, and it drew her into
a group of similarly glittering young investigators. One afternoon
she was sitting with them on a corner of the porch, facing a much-
needed breeze while gently mocking the hobbies and dumpy clothes
and general slackness of the older scientists. Where had their ambi-
tion gone? Their concentration?

"They go out *antiquing*," Elora said scornfully, which made
everyone laugh until a sunspotted face suddenly rose from the
ground below them. Then they were mortified, especially (the man
was Sebastian's advisor, who'd chosen Sebastian to be there: as
they'd each been chosen by someone old) when he tried to laugh off
what he'd overheard.

"So *cruel!*" he said. Ha ha ha. His waving hand resembled a bun-
dle of broken twigs. "Like a bunch of little wolves."

Rosalind smiled, before guiltily hiding her face. People she'd
known only vaguely for years suddenly wanted to talk with her;
strangers approached her at meals; a journalist from a general science magazine wanted her to write an article. All day she fizzed
around, catching up with Dee, who was having her own thrilling
success, whenever they could find each other. Afterwards, very late,
she met Sebastian.

His own talk, on how he'd determined the molecule responsible for the antimicrobial properties of a fungus found in Brazil,
had been poorly attended, but he claimed that this didn't bother
him; with the exception of his twig-fingered advisor, few people here

respected fieldwork or traditional knowledge and he didn't expect them to recognize what he'd done. While he played with her hair— they talked in bed, only in bed—he praised what he'd learned from amateur naturalists rooted in their environments. In Alaska, near Sitka, where he was headed as soon as the conference ended, an herbalist in an isolated forest had collected mycorrhizal fungi never before described. Some Hawaiian families cured infections with mycelium found under particular logs; on Baffin Island, explorers from the time of Franklin and his followers had studied a puffball supposed to cure stomach ailments.

Sometimes it was almost dawn before they fell asleep beneath the open window. Her exhaustion, she would have claimed, was caused by that simple lack of sleep, not by boredom or irritation. Not by the way old acquaintances asked her the same questions they'd asked the previous year and the year before that and aired the same grievances. Not by the other repetitions, or by the fierce, quiet quarrels taking place in the background, everyone competing for jobs and grants and fellowships. When she found herself gnaw- ing her knuckles, which she hadn't done since college, she blamed her busy schedule. Whatever discord she recognized could be eased, she found, simply by stepping outside. At night, the planets gleamed in the dark sky like luminescent fish. At dawn the field was sop- ping wet and every creature, including her, left long trails in the dew. Moss grew between the trees, other mosses grew on the trunks, lichens silently decomposed rocks as chickadees flicked from branch to branch. The afternoon sky produced troops of clouds above the serpentine path. Surrounding her were people she mostly liked, with minds as dazzling as the aspen leaves that flipped to expose their silver parts. Sometimes, in the early evening, they played croquet with broken mallets while hooting loudly. Why would a person ever leave such a place?

A young woman plopped down next to Rosalind after dinner one night, peering intently through long, narrow eyes set deep in their sockets. Her thick hair, dark red, grew over her ears and neck, reminding Rosalind of the fox she'd seen snatching mice from the edge of the meadow.

"You came to my talk!" the woman said. "I saw you in the audience."

Rosalind almost said, *Did I?* but managed, despite remembering nothing of it, to say, "I did." The talk had so resembled a hundred other talks that she could no longer recall a single point or even the title, only the relief of knowing she could let her mind wander. Why did the owlet she saw on the path around the pond make that remarkable noise? What was that flat red fungus extending like a Ping-Pong paddle from the hemlock? So much to investigate, but the work she did took all her time and every part of her brain. A narrowing of focus onto one crucial, difficult problem, posing questions that could be answered. What an odd way to spend a life.

The young woman, whose name was Kylie, described her research eagerly. She appeared again after another dinner, stressing how much Rosalind's work had inspired her, what an influence Rosalind had been. Again in the lobby after a panel; again at the lake. Praise like a fox tongue licking away, begging for a response; too slowly, Rosalind realized she wanted a favor.

Dee shrugged when, over breakfast, Rosalind described her unhappy insight. "Didn't you expect that?" Dee asked. "We used to do it too, telling someone what a huge influence he'd been, how his paper on whatever had changed everything." She gestured at the marmalade, which Rosalind pushed her way. "Except we did it with men, because there weren't any women around. Now," Dee added, coating her toast, "we're on the other side, is all."

From the porch outside came laughter and voices calling "Look,

look!" Dee rose, toast in hand, and Rosalind followed her through the lobby to the steps, where everyone in the crowd was staring east. An antique biplane flew over the trees, across the field, toward the colony, over all of them. "Oh!" cried Charlene, who'd leapt to the grass and, like a much younger woman, was waving both hands over her head.

"Every year," Dee said, and laughed.

"Every year," Rosalind agreed. Not far away was a private flying field that hosted an air show devoted to vintage planes, usually held at the same time as the conference. In a minute Charlene would say (and now she did say), "I think that's a Curtiss JN-4, a Jenny," and then describe the history of that WWI aircraft and the village on Crooked Lake, in central New York, where it had been built. Polite Dee, thoughtful Dee, would marvel as if this were news and ask Charlene the questions needed to propel her stories, so that the newest visitors could gaze, dazzled, at the remarkable plane and the woman who'd made it possible for them to see it.

Afterwards, walking alone in the hayfield (Dee and her new French friends were organizing a winter meeting in St. Bart's), for the first time Rosalind saw the field not as a fan but as a funnel, gathering up and concentrating onto the vine-shaded porches the whole world of science, the elaborate structure of meetings and speeches and grants and reputations she'd assumed was her home.

NEAR THE END of the meeting, another storm, stronger and more destructive than the first one, passed through. The candles and kerosene lamps they used when the lights went out seemed romantic; less so not being able to wash, as the well pumps didn't work without electricity. When they still lacked power the following night, Rosalind and Dee, along with her new French friends, Sebastian, and a few other young investigators, went down to the lake. They stripped, showing off in the moonlight, and hurled themselves into the water. Rosalind came up with streaks of mud on her arms, a stripe of blood running down one shin.

"Rock," she said. "Underwater."

Laughing as she said it. Dee tossed her a towel, and instead of covering herself, she whisked at her hair and then pressed the cloth to her bloody leg. Sebastian, who waded over to inspect the wound, said it was only a scratch and tossed the towel back to Dee before plastering Rosalind's shin with warm mud. When she saw the older scientists, the ones who'd taught her generation, watching from the edge of the woods, she didn't know enough to realize they might have done similar things when they were young. Some probably understood, as she did not, why she later left them.

I walked away from my first postdoc to do another in a completely different field, Marianne would write her afterwards. *I lost a couple of years, but it was worth it. You could have taken a leave and then started over—maybe with a different problem, something new. You might have done valuable—really valuable—science for another twenty-five years. Instead—*

Instead, some months after the conference ended and Rosalind and Sebastian split up (she'd known all along he was off to Alaska), Dee brought her the news of the caving accident. Rosalind had not thought about Sebastian much while she could still picture him working elsewhere. He might have traveled to another continent without letting her know, much as her sister used to do; he was somewhere working, that was fine. But now . . . for months after reading the obituary she continued on as if nothing had changed. Then, so swiftly and efficiently that even she was startled, she abandoned her lab in Chicago and the man who'd sent the postcard.

In the village where she'd been raised, she bought a house and adopted a tufty-headed gray dog, arranged new positions for people who'd worked in her lab, disposed of her old apartment. She bought a bed and a sofa and found a teaching job at a junior college on the shore of another lake. *Why?* people asked her. As if there was an answer. Even when Dee was doing the asking, all Rosalind could say was that she didn't know; that all her answers about herself were lies. She'd been lonely in her old life, or she felt engulfed, or she yearned or feared to belong to a group; she loved being absorbed by her work or hated the way that kept her from the larger world; she despised being flattered or needed it; she hurt some people or they hurt her; or the world changed or she changed or science changed or none of those things. So many hypotheses! A well-designed experiment offered a question posed correctly, to which an answer might be found. She had, simply, to do the experiment.

THE FAMILIES

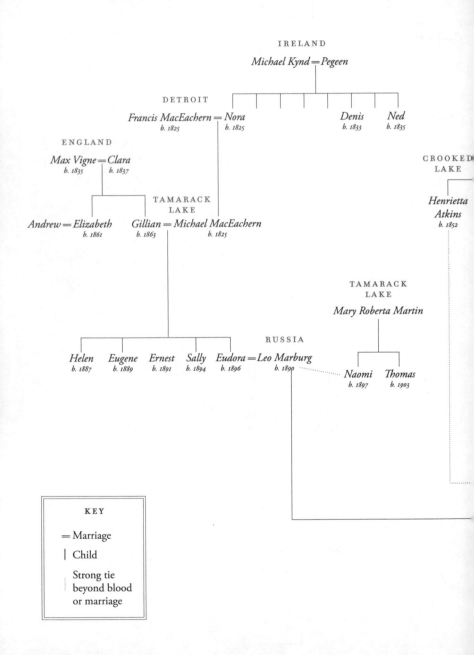

IRELAND

Michael Kynd = Pegeen

DETROIT

Francis MacEachern = Nora
b. 1825 — b. 1825

Denis — Ned
b. 1833 — b. 1835

ENGLAND

Max Vigne = Clara
b. 1835 — b. 1837

CROOKED
LAKE

Henrietta
Atkins
b. 1852

TAMARACK
LAKE

Andrew = Elizabeth — Gillian = Michael MacEachern
b. 1861 — b. 1863 — b. 1825

TAMARACK
LAKE

Mary Roberta Martin

RUSSIA

Helen — Eugene — Ernest — Sally — Eudora = Leo Marburg
b. 1887 — b. 1889 — b. 1891 — b. 1894 — b. 1896 — b. 1890

Naomi — Thomas
b. 1897 — b. 1903

KEY

= Marriage

| Child

Strong tie
beyond blood
or marriage

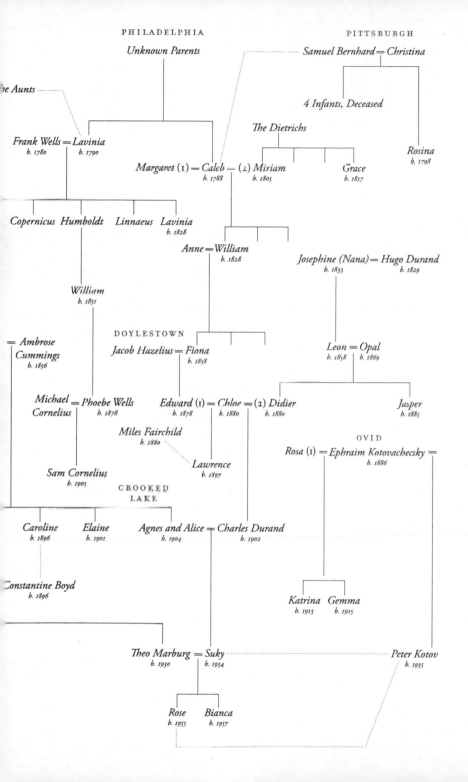

AUTHOR'S NOTE AND ACKNOWLEDGMENTS

In 1994, when I set a story called "The Marburg Sisters" in the central New York village of Hammondsport, I had no idea that I'd write more stories about those young women, nor that I'd spend several decades imagining generations of their family and friends. I took as a given, when I started, that Rose and Bianca were interested in science. Only much later, as the sisters' forebears came into focus, did I see the roots of their deep curiosity about the natural world.

As their history expanded, an imagined landscape encased the actual village, with which it shares steep hills, a long, narrow valley, a tiny airfield, and a handful of streets at the tip of a Y-shaped lake. In two novels and a number of stories, set in places ranging from the Arctic to Philadelphia to the Adirondacks, characters connected to Rose and Bianca go about their business, but the stories closest to them—especially "The Marburg Sisters," from *Ship Fever*; "The Mysteries of Ubiquitin" and "The Forest," from *Servants of the Map*; and "The Investigators" and "The Island," from *Archangel*—are all rooted in the place here called Crooked Lake.

Portions of this book have appeared previously, in somewhat different form, in the following publications: "Wonders of the Shore" in *Tin House* (Winter 2016) and in *The Best American Short Stories, 2016*; "The Regimental History" in *Ploughshares* (Fall 2019); "The

Accident" in *Harvard Review* (Winter 2016); and "Open House" in *American Short Fiction* (Fall 2016). I'm grateful to these publications and their editors.

Many thanks to my wonderful agent, Emily Forland, whose steady gaze helped this book find its final shape, and to my editor, Matt Weiland, who provided the best kind of encouragement and support. My deepest thanks, as always, to Margot Livesey, without whose friendship and brilliant guidance there would have been no book at all.